PRAISE FOR VIVI

"If you've never read a Vivian Arend book you are missing out on one of the best contemporary authors writing today."
~ *Book Reading Gals*

A Firefighter's Christmas Gift is a sweet romance; a heart-warming and passionate Christmas story. The premise is inspiring and delightful: the romance is encouraging and sensual.
~The Reading Cafe

This is a wonderful love story, and it was a magical Christmas story. It was great to celebrate the holiday with the residents of heart falls.
~ Book Addict Live

"This story will keep you reading from the first page to the last one. There is never a dull moment..."
~ *Landy Jimenez*

"I definitely recommend to fans of contemporaries with hot cowboys and strong family ties.."
~ *SmexyBooks*

"This was my first Vivian Arend story, and I know I want more!"
~ *Red Hot Plus Blue Reads*

Another masterpiece of love and passion Ms. Arend and all I have to say is THANK YOU!
~Romance Witch Reviews

ALSO BY VIVIAN AREND

Holidays in Heart Falls

A Firefighter's Christmas Gift

A Soldier's Christmas Wish

A Hero's Christmas Hope

A Cowboy's Christmas List

A Rancher's Christmas Kiss

The Stones of Heart Falls

A Rancher's Heart

A Rancher's Song

A Rancher's Bride

A Rancher's Love

A Rancher's Vow

The Colemans of Heart Falls

The Cowgirl's Forever Love

The Cowgirl's Secret Love

The Cowgirl's Chosen Love

Heart Falls Vignette Collection

Three Weddings and a Baby

A full list of Vivian's print titles is available on her website

www.vivianarend.com

A HERO'S CHRISTMAS HOPE

HOLIDAYS IN HEART FALLS: BOOK 3

VIVIAN AREND

This is a work of fiction. Names, characters, places, and incidents either are the product of the author's imagination or are used fictitiously, and any resemblance to any persons, living or dead, business establishments, events, or locales is entirely coincidental.

A Hero's Christmas Hope

ISBN: 9781989507155
Edited by Anne Scott
Cover Design © Damonza
Proofed by Angie Ramey, Linda Levy, & Manuela Velasco

FOREWORD

This book was written during a challenging time in our shared history. Lockdowns, protests, families separated for a multitude of reasons.

Life is not the same...yet we will get through.

Perhaps your holiday traditions have been thrown out the window. Even as we acknowledge our sorrow, let's celebrate the opportunity to make new traditions that are even better. Let go of what's not serving you and your loved ones. Find new ways to share joy.

Holiday magic can make amazing things happen.

1

December 1, somewhere on Highway 22x, Alberta

Madison Joy cranked up the volume right as the drum solo hit, the deep bass reverberating throughout the interior of her car. She bopped her head decisively, dancing in her seat even as she resisted the urge to play a set of air drums.

As much fun as wielding invisible drumsticks would be, darkness had fallen hours ago, and with the iffy winter road conditions, two hands on the wheel was a far smarter idea.

Satisfying the urge to move by continuing to wiggle enthusiastically, she peeked at the expected arrival time on the GPS.

“Woo-hoo. Look at that. ‘Less than twenty minutes from your destination.’”

Headlights appeared over the hill as a truck barreled toward her. Its lights flicked from high to low a second later than they should’ve, and Madison’s eyes watered as she narrowed her gaze against the glare.

Nighttime driving had never been her thing. Or maybe she

was just reaching her limit for the day. Considering it was a thirteen-hour drive from Vancouver to Heart Falls, she'd been on the road since very early that morning.

Still, one entire audiobook and a whole lot of music had helped pass the time, and now she was closing in on the next important part of her new adventure.

Madison turned down the music and sighed happily as she relaxed into her seat. Ten years ago, her college education had been cut short when her dad was killed in an accident and her mom fell into a deep, dark depression. With two much-younger brothers potentially being dropped into social services, Madison had stepped in and taken over raising them.

She never regretted it, but now that they were grown up and her mom was doing well, it was time to move on.

Her phone went off, and she hit answer via Bluetooth. "Miss me?" she asked Little Brother Number One.

"Never." At eighteen, Joe's voice still edged into youthful innocence at times. "Since you told me not to text while you were driving, I had to call. Where'd you hide the air popper?"

"Oh, so you can live without me but not your popcorn?"

"Damn right," he agreed.

"Joseph Maxwell Joy, no swearing in this house."

Madison snickered as her mother's voice rang in the background. "Yeah, Joseph. No swearing," Madison teased.

He laughed. "Any ideas on the popper, Mad?"

"Try the front hall closet," she suggested. "What are you guys watching tonight?"

"Kyle wants to start a Lord of the Rings marathon."

"Again? And on a Tuesday night?" Good grief. "Well, thankfully I'm not there to have to join you."

"But you totally would have, and you'd have ended up reciting every Gandalf speech verbatim, so thanks for not being here and making us witness that. *Again*."

"Brat."

"Found the popper. Front closet." Joe lowered his voice. "And don't tell anyone else, but I do miss you. But we're all glad you're gone—not only because I'm taking over your room, but because you deserve to have some fun."

"Yeah, driving cross-Canada is going to be a blast," she drawled. "Saskatchewan will be a thrill a minute."

"Who's the brat now?"

She laughed. "Give Mom a hug, punch Kyle for me, and call me again, but not until tomorrow. Jeez, you're so needy."

"Love ya, Mad." He hung up, leaving her with a warm glow of happiness inside.

She could picture the activity at home. Her mom had obviously hauled the second of her eighteen-year-old twins in to help clean up after dinner. Joe would make an enormous batch of popcorn, and all of them would crowd around the TV. Impossibly long, teenage-boy legs would be propped up on the coffee table. Butter and salt scents on the air, and the movie turned up loud enough to make the walls vibrate.

Home.

Madison might have poked Joe about missing her already, but the truth was the knot in her belly said she was the one feeling left out. Which was a terrible and weird thing, since she also felt happy and excited.

Emotions were so damn complicated.

While she'd been talking with Joe, the light hint of snow had thickened. It whipped past her window, huge flakes catching in the headlights and turning the road ahead into a blur.

She caught herself mid-sigh, the noise turning into something between a hiccup and a laugh. Time for a pep talk.

"You're headed to see one of your best friends in the whole wide world, and you got another full month before you start your new job. From where you're sitting, life is looking fine."

Bonus: her GPS announced she was closing in on her final destination.

She'd never been to Ryan's house in Heart Falls, but she wasn't worried about not being welcomed. They might have fallen out of touch over the past couple of years, but their friendship was rock-solid. Forever friends, that's what they were.

They'd pinkie-sworn on it and everything back when they were twelve.

Still, she'd booked a motel for a couple of weeks so she could visit in the spare moments he could give her. She hadn't wanted to announce she was coming, just in case she'd had to call it off at the last minute.

Something in the back seat began buzzing. Or rather, something inside one of the boxes stacked in her back seat. She'd never been a pack rat. It hadn't taken long to bundle everything she owned into the car with room to spare. And one of those things was now making excited noises.

Madison reached back to blindly bang on the cardboard in the hopes it would stop.

Of course, the instant her attention wasn't fully on the road, she missed the warning for the right-hand turn she was supposed to make.

Heart Falls was small enough that there were no overhead streetlights this far from the center of town. She was stuck on a dark, narrow swatch of pavement that seemed to curve around the shadowy silhouettes of the buildings to her right. Nothing was visible to her left except wide-open fields and, in the far distance, the shadowy outlines of the Rocky Mountains.

"Please a legal U-turn make," her GPS requested in a familiar nasal tone.

Yoda as a copilot usually amused her, but right now Madison would just like to get where she was going, thank you very much.

She slowed, looking for a place to make that legal U-turn, and her tires slipped. An adjustment to the steering wheel had no effect on her vehicle. She tapped her brakes, but nothing.

Forward motion continued, the car sliding farther to the right, and Madison swore. She wasn't going to be able to fix this in time. Madison braced both hands on the wheel as her front passenger tire hit the ditch, and her vehicle left the highway.

As her car bumped madly over the uneven ground, she tugged the wheel from side to side, guiding her descent as best she could. A gentle slide instead of a straight plummet seemed like a good idea. Fortunately, there were no trees or massive rocks in her way. Or at least none that she could see in the limited illumination offered by her headlights.

A barbed wire fence shot into view, offering barely any resistance as her Honda Civic smashed through it. Wires snapped, the loose strands scraping against the car's paint job like fingernails on a chalkboard.

When the vehicle jostled to a stop, Madison gasped for air. Other than her heart pounding in her ears loud enough to deafen her, everything, including her, seemed to be in one piece.

She leaned back in the seat and tried to calm—

The steering wheel airbag went off, smashing into her with breakneck speed, stealing a scream from her as pain shot to high.

So much for her luck holding.

UP ON THE HIGHWAY, Ryan Zhao parked his truck as far to the edge of the asphalt as possible and hit the hazard lights. The wind just about took his door off the frame, snow crystals slamming against his skin as he quickly but cautiously made his way across the road and into the ditch.

Snow flickered in front of his flashlight. The icy-cold December wind stole his breath as he waded through the tall, dry grass barely touched with the recent inch of snowfall.

What a contrast. Less than thirty minutes ago, it had been absolutely calm, and he'd been sitting in quiet contemplation in the Heart Falls cemetery. With his ten-year-old daughter, Talia, out for the night at a friend's, he'd taken the evening to do some serious thinking.

And while his wife, Justina, wasn't buried in the small community graveyard, Ryan had a habit of going there when he wanted to honour her memory. When he needed to think.

When he needed to make decisions.

He'd left the cemetery with a new goal in mind, but all of that was swept away as he focused on the potential disaster he was striding toward.

The red taillights on the car in front of him faded as the engine cut out, and Ryan picked up the pace. He tapped his pocket to make sure his phone was still there. As a coordinator with the Heart Falls volunteer fire department, he was one of the best people to act as first responder at the scene.

Still, no matter his training, the sight of a bloody handprint on the inside of the driver's window shot adrenaline through his system. He peered inside and spotted a single figure slouched behind the wheel, motionless. "Hey. I'm here to help. I'm going to open the door—don't move."

A woman groaned loudly then swore as the cold wind whipped into the passenger space. "Dammit, that hurt like hell."

The deployed airbag was one clue, but Ryan wasn't going to make any assumptions. He pressed a hand to her shoulder to keep her in place. "Don't move for a minute. Let's make sure it's safe to get you out of there."

"Ryan?"

Her voice sounded far too familiar, and the fact she knew

his name meant he needed to take a closer look. But first—"*Don't move* means your head as well. You've been in a car crash. You might have a neck injury."

"I didn't crash," she insisted. "But holy hell, that airbag packs a punch. My teeth feel like they're loose. Is my wrist still attached to my arm? My fingers are numb."

He made sure the car was solid before doing anything else. It was firmly wedged in position, so he leaned in to do a quick check on the woman's neck and shoulders. That put him face-to-face with a bleeding nose, reddish-brown hair, and a pair of familiar bright-green eyes.

"What are you doing, Madison Joy?" Ryan asked without really expecting an answer, but she gave one anyway.

"Bleeding?" She ran her tongue over her teeth. "*Yay* for safety systems, but damn it, my nose hurts."

Her voice had gone nasal as the swelling accelerated. Ryan eyed the inside of the vehicle, but the lack of any other damage plus the position of the car seemed to follow her claim of not having any impact injuries. "Let's undo your seat belt and get you out of there."

"My hero," Madison mumbled. "Back up a bit so I can swing my legs out. Then you can give me all the help you want."

The tattered remains of the airbag were pushed aside, and Madison twisted toward him with a groan. She offered her right hand, cradling her left against her chest, and an instant later, she was standing, Ryan's arm around her back.

She swayed briefly, but he held her in place until she patted his arm. "Just a bit of a head rush. Honest, nothing hurts too bad except for not being able to take a deep breath. And my wrist feels as if it was stepped on by an elephant. They weren't lying when they said those damn airbags can be nearly as dangerous as being in an accident without them."

"I don't think your nose is broken," Ryan told her. "But we'll get them to take a look at it in Emergency. Your wrist as well.

Arms and wrists are the other things that usually get damaged."

She snorted then groaned. "Ouch. Remind me not to do that again." She touched her nose gingerly then attempted another tentative body shimmy. "I think my ribs are okay. The boobs, on the other hand, are feeling rather tender. Like after a good old groping."

It was Ryan's turn to snicker, guiding her back up the embankment toward his truck. "I'll take your word on that."

"Hey, a good groping can be a lot of fun," Maddy insisted. "Fooling around with an airbag, a little less so."

The wind was shrieking by now, but Ryan took his time. He got her safely to the side of his truck and into the passenger seat. He buckled her up before closing the door.

By the time he got behind the wheel, Madison had flipped down the sun visor and opened the mirror and light to examine her face. "Well, shit." She turned to face him, her pale skin nearly grey under the feeble interior light. Blood from her nose had smeared her cheeks, turning her into a rather gory sight. Still, she managed a smile and, in a perky voice, announced, "Hi, Ryan. I've come for a visit."

"Seriously?"

"I would've called, but then it wouldn't have been a surprise." She made a horrible face, wiggling her jaw before reaching up to double-check her front teeth. She glanced at him. "You surprised?"

"A little. A lot." Ryan carefully pulled out onto the highway. "Hospital?"

She took a deep breath then wiggled in her seat. "I assume you're still first-aid certified. So am I. I do *not* have any broken ribs. The nose, probably not either. Everything else is just bruises and adrenaline at this point. Damn airbag," she grumbled before glancing over at him. "Skip the hospital. Just take me to my motel. I'll get cleaned up so I don't scare your daughter."

"You're not staying at a motel." It wasn't a question. "I have a spare room at my place. You won't scare Talia once you no longer look as if you've gone ten rounds in the ring. Besides, she's not home tonight, so there's time for you to get showered up."

"There we go. That means I finally get to see your home sweet home here in Heart Falls." She relaxed back in her seat, still making little stretching motions and groaning as she moved. "I was so close to making it in one piece."

"We'll deal with your car tomorrow," he promised before glancing to the side. "You okay otherwise? I mean, is there a reason for the surprise visit other than curiosity or old time's sake?"

She breathed deep and let it out slowly. "Mostly it's a visit because you're my friend, and I've missed you. And we did say that anytime, anywhere, we could drop in on each other."

She was totally up to something. "We did say that," Ryan agreed. "Spill the beans, Maddy. What sent you to me, car full of everything you own?"

"Change of circumstances," she admitted. "I'll tell you the rest of it after I've washed the blood off. But it's nothing terrible, I promise."

Which meant Ryan could relax a little, because the one thing Madison had never done was lie to him. So, whatever weird bullshit had happened to send her back into his world out of the blue, it wasn't dire.

Which meant he could focus on driving the short distance to his home on the outskirts of Heart Falls.

Madison Joy. His best friend throughout junior high and high school. Heck, his best friend for the first couple of years of college before she'd had to leave school suddenly. She was the one who introduced him to his wife, Justina.

Madison might not have been around much for the last ten years, but they'd kept in touch off and on. Having her back seemed strangely right.

Ryan pulled into his driveway.

She leaned forward to look up at the mostly dark outline of his home. "Cute place, far as I can see."

He parked the truck in front of the garage and gestured toward the entrance. "Come on. Let's check out the damage so you can get washed up."

2

Ryan led her into a very tidy kitchen area with a small island across from the stove, and the window over the sink looked out over darkness. A few steps to the right, four chairs were pushed in around a small wooden table, and the entire kitchen was a blur of honey-coloured wood.

He paused at the sink, soaking a cloth before handing it to her. "Here. That should feel good before I start poking to confirm the rest of you is only bent, not broken."

She groaned as the heat from the soft cloth set her nerve endings tingling. "Not good, fantastic."

He gave her a moment to clean up. Once she'd use the cloth a half dozen times, squeezing it clean between each round, Ryan gave her a quick and efficient once-over. He manipulated her fingers, shoulders, and arms then checked her legs and hips without once cracking a smile. His focused examination gave her time to look him over and once again gawk at how gloriously well put together he was.

Having him as a best friend for all those years had been like getting to hang around with a movie star. Girls watched him, staring or flirting madly if they got the opportunity. Madison didn't blame them one bit.

His dark hair was just a little longer than she remembered, the blue-black strands curling slightly behind his ears. His dark-brown eyes focused intently as he checked her pupils, the flashlight in his hand making her eyes water until she had to blink.

"Thanks. Now I'm seeing stars," Madison said in mock complaint.

"You might be seeing stars through two black eyes by the morning," he warned. "But your nose isn't broken, and neither is your wrist."

He pulled off his sweater, draping it over the back of the kitchen chair beside him. He moved to roll up his shirt sleeves, and Madison paused in the middle of wiping the final bit of blood from the back of her wrists with the warm washcloth.

His forearms moved in a mesmerizing dance, the muscles underneath rippling under firm copper-brown skin. In spite of the pain still drifting through various parts of her, the sight of those forearms was better than any medication.

"I'm going to check your ribs," Ryan warned, stepping behind her. "You okay with that?"

She tossed the washcloth into the sink then stretched her arms to the sides. "Do your worst."

"Tell me if anything hurts." He placed both hands on her hips. Slowly, he worked his way up, pressing gently as he moved over her waist, the base of her ribs, then higher.

His thumbs brushed the underside of her arm, and she fought to keep from wiggling.

Ryan froze. "Did that hurt?"

"Ticklish," she said in a rush. She wasn't going to mention the fact that she was on fire because his hands were on her. She wasn't that starved for touch—

Who was she kidding? It'd been so long since anyone else had touched her other than platonic family hugs.

Ryan was a wall of heat behind her, one hand on the front of her rib cage, the other on her back. "Take a deep breath," he ordered.

She breathed in, and he applied pressure. The twinges of pain were there but nowhere near worrisome.

"The ribs are fine," she said. "What I feel are damaged muscles. Definitely bruised."

"One more check."

He adjusted position to test her other side, but Madison was happy to offer the same report. "Ribs are good. But I bet we can play connect-the-dots with my bruises in a day or two and discover whole new constellations."

"I've got arnica cream somewhere," he promised. "Okay, you're clear to get washed up. Come on. You'll feel better once the blood is gone."

They moved too quickly for her to be able to admire the rest of the house, but the bathroom he guided her to had more than enough going for it. Ryan pointed to the cupboard on the opposite side of the space.

"Extra supplies are in there. You'll find a toothbrush and whatever else you need. Oh, and wait a second." He left the room but was back before she'd had time to do more than turn on the water in the shower to let it start heating. He laid a pile of clothes beside the sink then offered a grin. "We'll get the rest of your stuff later, but for now, this will do."

"Thank you," she said earnestly. "For everything. This wasn't the grand entrance I was hoping to make."

"Friends are always welcome," Ryan assured her. "And old friends are especially good to see, grand entrance or not." He gestured toward the shower where steam was starting to billow. "Enjoy yourself. I'll get some food ready for when you're done, and we can get caught up."

Madison stood under the scalding hot water and let it pour over her face. Her nose throbbed in a dull beat, and she agreed she'd probably have at least a hint of black eyes, but otherwise she was pretty much unscathed.

She might not have gotten off scot-free, but all things considered, she was grateful to have been so lucky.

And now, here she was. Invading on Ryan, with all sorts of thoughts running through her brain. Thoughts she didn't know if she had the right to have.

He was even more attractive than she remembered.

Distracting herself with shampoo and soap, Madison scrubbed herself clean before buffing dry in the sinfully soft towel Ryan had laid out for her.

The clothing he'd left included a tank top as well as a button-down shirt and a pair of sweatpants she had to roll up at the ankles a couple of times so she wouldn't trip over them.

A quick glance in the mirror as she dragged a comb through her hair said the damages were less than expected. Her nose was only a third beyond its normal size. There were no other bruises on her face, although some were already rising on her chest, especially where the seat belt had crossed her body.

The smell of something salty and savoury dragged her from the bathroom and back into the kitchen. "Oh, God. Did you make ramen?"

Ryan grinned at her over his shoulder, ladling broth into two bowls. "What kind of a friend would I be if I didn't make your favourite meal?"

"One who wasn't expecting said friend to literally drop in." She joined him at the table that was already set for two. "Thank you."

At her side, Ryan dipped his chin, and then they both fell quiet for a moment, the flavourful broth taking all of her attention. She was more than halfway done before realizing she'd been snarfing down the food like one of her teenage brothers.

Ryan's eyes danced with amusement when she met his stare and offered a gentle, "Oops?"

He lifted noodles even as he assured her, "I'm just as hungry. And soup is nice when you're cold inside."

"Thank you for rescuing me," she said sincerely. "I'm very glad you just happened to be on that stretch of highway."

Ryan waved a hand. "I'm very glad your rescue involved not much more than a quick walk down a hill and a hot shower." He checked his watch. "You know, it's early enough that we might be able to get your stuff out of the ditch tonight."

"That would be handy. It's not that I'm worried about anything valuable going missing, but it would be nice to have my things." She remembered something else. "Are you sure about me staying here tonight?"

"Tonight and longer if you want. I've got the room." Ryan paused for a moment. "You need to—"

"I should cancel my motel," Madison said at the same moment, and they smiled at each other. "Great minds think alike?"

"Looks that way. You have your phone?"

"Yep. Just give me a minute." She pulled it out and hit a few buttons. "It's late, so I'll probably pay for tonight, but at least this way they won't be expecting me to show up."

Ryan rose to grab more broth for them while Madison chatted with the woman at the motel. By the time he had their bowls topped up, she had a full refund and a laugh to share.

She pointed a finger at him. "So. Tell me about your dating life."

He stopped in the middle of swallowing a noodle, choking slightly before he could speak again. "Excuse me?"

From the innocent look of shock on his face, it was clearly

high school and college all over again. The man had no idea exactly how attractive he was.

Madison leaned back in her chair and grinned. "Darla down at the Heart Falls motel said there was no problem making the cancellation, but could I please be sure to tell Ryan that she had *soooo* much fun at the square dance last month."

Ryan mouthed the name, confusion folding his firm brow. "No idea who that—oh. Oh, *her*."

"The mystery thickens." Madison wanted to know everything that had been going on in her friend's life. Which she had assumed, after all these years, probably involved some special woman. "From that response, I assume she's not someone you're seeing regularly?"

Ryan raised a brow. "Oh, I see her regularly. My bar, Rough Cut, is a happening place for the singles in the Heart Falls area. Which means everyone from the hands at the local ranches, construction crews from the highway maintenance and the new oil fields to the south, and a whole lot of ladies—including a few in their late fifties and early sixties."

"Ah, a little bit of Mrs. Robinson."

He leaned forward on his elbows and made direct eye contact. "I make it a rule to not date anyone old enough to be my mother."

Stomach filling with good food, her entire body warming up, Madison gave in to her curiosity and examined what she could see of the house.

The kitchen and dining area were flanked by a narrow hallway leading to the bedroom area and a living room with a couch and two easy chairs. A wide coffee table rested in the center of the comfortable space. The wall opposite the front door held a computer desk and two tall bookcases, one covered with framed pictures and the other books, magazines, and tidy storage containers.

Two cardboard boxes labelled *Christmas decorations* were stacked to one side. Probably getting ready to be put up.

She leapt back into the conversation. "I want to get caught up on everything, but we may as well keep this topic going. Are you dating?"

Ryan made a face. "Honestly? Not yet. But—" He stirred the few remaining noodles in his bowl with his chopsticks, staring into the broth. "Before I came across you in the ditch, I was down at the local cemetery. I go there when I want to have time to think. I just tonight decided I might be ready to try again."

He said it with such reluctance that Madison couldn't stop herself. She laid a hand on his arm. "Good for you. And you don't need my permission, but I'll say it anyway. I know how much you loved Justina, but I'm pretty sure she'd want this for you."

An enormous sigh escaped him. "I still miss her."

"Of course, you do," Madison said sincerely. "So do I, and I was only a friend. She was very special."

Madison had done the mental math before she came out here. She'd been shocked to realize it had been nearly eight years since Ryan's wife had died unexpectedly. A brain aneurysm had come out of the blue and taken her quickly.

For a moment, the two of them sat in silence before Ryan laid a hand on top of Madison's and squeezed her knuckles. He offered a soft smile. "Sorry, that was a sobering way to kill a reconnection moment."

Madison blew a raspberry at his apologetic tone. "Hotshot, it doesn't matter that it's been years since I saw you in person. We're ride-or-die friends. Ride-or-die friends don't ever apologize."

~

It was easy to smile around Madison. Blunt, down to earth. Pretty much the same girl he'd met that first summer day when she climbed over the back fence between their yards and they promptly got into trouble.

Only, he had to roll his eyes. "Dear God, I have not heard that nickname in forever."

"Hotshot?" Madison's smile turned visibly evil. "Really? Nobody here knows what a wild man you are?"

Ryan straightened slightly, deliberately cool and collected. "I'll have you know I'm a fine, upstanding member of the community. Member of the Chamber of Commerce, team leader for the Heart Falls volunteer fire department."

"Bar owner." She winked at him. "Not that I'll give you any grief for that, but I bet some of the more conservative folk do a little pearl clutching when you're around."

"I'm also the co-chair of the local food bank. We took over from the local churches because they couldn't get enough volunteers," Ryan offered dryly. "We pretty much get along in this town. There are moments it's pretty rustic, and there're a lot of deals done with nothing more than a handshake and a nod. But the pace of life feels pretty good."

Madison looked thoughtful for a moment then dipped her chin decisively. "Good for you. Sounds idyllic, and a great place to raise a kid." Then her expression turned eager. "Tell me about Talia. She's got to be so big now."

"Growing so fast. She's amazing. Ten, going on eleven in a few weeks. Grade four, so I can still manage to help with her homework." Just the thought of his daughter triggered that spot in his heart filled with joy and trepidation. Everything he did was for her—to see her grow and bloom the way he and Justina had dreamed about since before Talia was born.

The idea of failing his daughter scared him even as it motivated him to try harder. Lately it was clear Talia trembled on the verge of changing from a little girl into a young woman, and there were so many potential potholes in the road ahead, he had no idea how he'd manage.

He hadn't realized that he'd gotten lost in his thoughts until his bowl and chopsticks were pulled from his hand. Madison winked as she headed to the sink and started on dishes.

He joined her. "Sorry. I'm obviously out of practice at friend-talk time."

"Well, let's keep practicing so you can remember how this works." Madison pushed him aside and stepped in front of the sink. "You know where things go. Dry and put them away."

"Yes, ma'am."

She snickered as she got to work on the washing. "You've been in Heart Falls for five years?"

He thought back briefly. "Nearly seven. After Justina died, Talia and I moved in with my parents, remember? Once I graduated, I moved us all out here. There's an attached in-law suite."

Madison glanced over her shoulder, leaning the direction he pointed. "I'm so glad you have their help."

"Me too. I couldn't have survived otherwise. They aren't there anymore, though."

"What?" Maddy held onto the ceramic bowl she was passing him, concern rising in her green eyes. "They moved out? Last I heard, they were living with you. They're still okay?"

"Yes. Dad's got diabetes, though, and he needs extra monitoring on a regular basis. Mom never learned to drive, and as Dad's eyesight has gotten worse, they decided it was better to live closer to the hospital and the doctor who treats him so they can bus or take a taxi to appointments." Ryan shook his head. "I thought about moving with them to Black Diamond—it's just over an hour from here—but Talia has good friends I didn't want to take her away from. Plus, I have both the part-time firefighting and the bar..."

Sometimes he still thought he'd made the wrong decision,

not being there for his parents the way he should be. But he simply couldn't move Talia from the people she'd grown up with. Not after she'd already lost her mom so young.

Ryan took Maddy on a quick tour of the house, pausing to swing open the door on the far-right wall. The narrow passage held a washer/dryer, and a door on the other side was the connection between the main house and the suite. "My babysitter rents the in-law suite. Laura has a regular nine-to-five at the lawyer's office, but with her on-site, she gets to sleep at home with the doors open the nights I'm on duty at the fire hall."

"I expected you to say she's here the evenings you're at the bar," Madison confessed.

It'd taken a lot of juggling to get things to this point, but so far it was working. "I work Rough Cut a few days, plus Friday and Saturday nights when Talia is at my parents' for the weekend. I'm running on the principle that I might own the place, but I shouldn't be indispensable. I've got a really good assistant manager I brought on a few months ago. Things are finally where if either one of my jobs has an emergency, I can jump in or not, depending on how things are set up with Talia."

"Sounds like a balancing act you're winning."

It was tempting to leave it at that, but Ryan had to let her know. "I love running the bar, but you always told me to do what made me happy. And firefighting, being part of a team, does. So it's been worth the effort to add that on."

She paused, head tilted to the side. "I said that?"

"Many times. Until it echoed in my brain," he offered dryly before tilting his head toward the hall. "Come on, finish poking around."

Peeking into Talia's room, Madison made an appropriately excited noise at the sight of the loft bed, but Ryan noticed the longer the tour went on, the closer *he* was being examined.

"What?" he demanded, half laughing.

Madison shrugged. "I'm trying to be polite."

"Oh, please. Like you're not dying to simply spit out exactly what's on your mind." It might have been years, but that was Maddy to the core.

She pushed past him into the master bedroom and was now pointing at his bed. "You're kidding me. What the hell is that?"

Ryan sighed. "It's a bed, Maddy."

"For a kid." She whirled on him. "Let me guess. When you moved in with your parents, you were in the same room as Talia, so two single beds were the limit."

"Right." He didn't say anything about not being able to stand to keep the queen-size mattress Justina and he had shared.

Madison sniffed at his neatly made twin that was pushed up against the far wall under the window, leaving a wide expanse of open carpet. "I guess this setup gives you room to do workouts at home, or some such nonsense."

"Yup."

She stalked across to his bathroom and peeked in, her expression brightening slightly. "At least you couldn't mess up this room. Nice huge shower, dude. And that soaker tub is probably great after a callout."

"Which reminds me. One second while I make a call."

"Don't mind me. I'm going to snoop through your closets, looking for more skeletons." Madison gave his bed one more disgusted glance, shook her head, then left the room.

It shouldn't take long to arrange for her car to be pulled from the ditch. "Hey, Mack. Got a minute?"

Having a best friend married to a mechanic was handy.

"We're just hanging out. What's up?" Mack asked.

"Does your lovely wife have time to tow a car out of the ditch?" Ryan asked. "I have a friend visiting who had a bit of bad luck on the Nelson corner. If Brooke can't do it tonight, tomorrow will be fine."

"One second, and I'll pass you over." Mack spoke in the background, and then suddenly it was a female voice on the line.

"You want us to bring the car to the shop or your house?" Brooke asked.

"If it's running, the house. It'll need a new airbag installed, but for now, it would be good if Madison could grab what she needs. I'm pretty sure the keys are in the ignition."

Brooke laughed. "You really think a little thing like no keys would stop me? Please."

Ryan caught himself grinning as he stepped back into his living room. "I know Mack is off tonight, so you guys should stay for a while. I'll introduce you to Madison."

"Deal. Shouldn't take more than an hour," Brooke promised.

Maddy was in front of the fridge, eyeing the calendar attached with brightly coloured magnets when he gave her the update.

Her eyes sparkled. "Thanks for taking care of me."

"That's what friends do," Ryan insisted.

She nodded then made a face. "Can I have a hug?"

Damn. It hadn't been a normal greeting from the start, but he was shocked that it had taken this long for her to ask.

Madison was a hugger.

Ryan didn't answer, just opened his arms.

She stepped against him and curled her arms around his torso, nestling in like it was years ago and miles away. A place where they'd watched each other's backs and given each other exactly what they needed. Friends who cared about the little details and the big ones.

He held her carefully, worried about squeezing her bruises too tight, but as their breathing synchronized, heat wrapping around them like a cozy blanket, it wasn't just him giving to her anymore.

His soul felt lighter knowing Maddy was here. That she cared enough to ask about his daughter, his parents, to notice his single bed.

She gave to him so easily in a brief time—it had to be that ride-or-die friendship she'd mentioned, and he was so grateful she'd dropped in out of the blue.

Eventually, Maddy patted his back. "Thanks. I needed that."

"Me too," Ryan confessed. He kissed her forehead, same as he'd do to Talia, then gestured Madison toward the living room. "Let's relax until your car gets here."

"Goodie." Maddy stole the calendar off the fridge then settled on the couch, motioning him over. "*Relax* means 'Ryan gets to tell Mad how long she's allowed to hang around and bug him'. Because I don't want to overstay my welcome."

Ryan sat in the armchair across from her. Not because he was uncomfortable sitting beside her but because she always did this. Whatever magic Madison Joy possessed turned people into blabbermouths.

They'd jokingly labelled it the bartender gene.

It was true that many in their field had the ability to make total strangers up and spill their most intimate secrets in a shockingly short period of time. Only it wasn't supposed to be that way between *them*.

Best friends, yet somehow the entire conversation over the past hour and a bit had been ninety percent about him. His life, his daughter, and his parents. His history.

He met her gaze straight on. "Put the calendar down, Maddy."

"But we need to plan," she insisted.

"We need to talk," he returned before correcting himself. "*You* need to talk. You haven't told me a single thing beyond you decided to come for a visit."

She hesitated. "Oh, right." A decisive nod followed. "It's not that I'm trying to hide anything, really," she said sincerely, "but

I did show up unannounced. You're too nice a guy to tell me to take a hike, so let's nail down the details now, and then I can relax."

That made sense. "You have all your stuff in your car." He raised a brow as he watched her, silently encouraging her to fill in the gaps.

Madison sighed. "I have a job in Toronto starting January fifth. So I need to head out early enough to make it without driving like an accident waiting to happen. I figured I'd stick around Heart Falls for two weeks, staying in a motel, then leave before the holidays so I'm not in the way."

"Nice try." For a second, Ryan's temper flashed. Where was she planning on spending the holidays? Alone in some motel room? "Forget the two-week thing. Also, forget the motel bullshit. You're staying with me and Talia for the entire time, and that's final."

"But I—" She slammed her lips together, took a deep breath, then dipped her chin. "Fine. No, not fine. *Wonderful.* Thank you, and that's awesome, and I am so looking forward to it. But just so you know? If I stay, I have a few fix-it items I'd like to play with. Don't say no."

3

Ryan's face was priceless in that moment. Madison leaned back on the couch and crossed one ankle over the other. "Is it a deal?"

He folded his arms. "Is this *fixer* thing of yours still as obnoxious as it was back in high school?"

"It's even better," Madison shared. "Or worse, I suppose, depending."

A snort escaped him. "Oh, great. That made total sense."

"Doesn't need to make sense," she pointed out. "You just need to agree to do the things I suggest."

Ryan shook his head, but he wasn't disagreeing with her. "Let me get a drink. If you plan on reorganizing my life, I need a bracer." He rose to his feet. "What do you want?"

"Ginger ale."

He nodded without questioning her choice and headed to the kitchen.

Her phone buzzed in her pocket, and she pulled it out to discover it was her other brother.

"Hey, brat," she said easily, watching Ryan move in the kitchen. "I thought you were visiting Middle Earth tonight."

"Intermission," Kyle said in a low whisper. "Hey, just wanted to let you know everything's okay."

A deep sense of relief welled up, but Madison fought to keep it from her voice. "Of course it is. You know between Aragon and Gandalf, things will be fine. And don't discount Samwise—"

"I know, I know. I need to read the book because Samwise is never an asshole or mean to Smeagol. The book is better than the movie, and all the rest of it." He mock-gagged.

"Actually, the movie and the book are equally great and terrible for different reasons. Pick the one you enjoy the most." Madison mouthed *thank you* at Ryan as he put a glass on the table in front of her. "Thanks for the update, bud. Anything else you need?"

"Nah. I'm glad you're gone. I'm taking over your room tomorrow," Kyle shared.

That was a disaster she was happy to miss—the twins fighting over her teeny room. "You do realize that your current room is way bigger than mine, especially if Joe moves out."

"Yours has a window that doesn't face the back alley."

"Happy fighting, then," Madison said. "I'm at Ryan's. Gotta go, 'kay?"

"Okay. Can I call you tomorrow?" Kyle asked it really soft and fast.

Her brothers were going to break her damn heart. She answered him gruffly so she didn't push him further toward tears, which would totally embarrass him, even with them so many miles apart. "I guess. Now go away."

"Love ya." He was gone even as she whispered *I love you* back.

Ryan watched silently. She wiggled her phone then dropped it on the table and grabbed her glass. "My brothers are making sure that I haven't forgotten how to use technology in the few hours since I left."

His face softened. "How are they?"

"Great," she said cheerfully. "They're both at the university, if you can believe it."

"Damn, already?"

"Time passes. Just like Talia's magically ten, the boys hit eighteen. Bonus, in the past couple of years, they finally figured out how to hand in assignments on time. Which will be helpful going forward."

The doorbell rang. Ryan frowned but rose to answer it.

She followed after him, peering over his shoulder to discover a very solidly built man with dark hair standing on the front stairs. A tall woman with a ponytail was climbing down from the tow truck parked on the street outside Ryan's house.

"Hey, Mack. Brooke." A trace of shock tinged Ryan's voice. She leaned out a little father and spotted her car, the paint job a little worse for wear, still attached behind the truck. "How did you get it out of the ditch that fast?"

The brunette sidled up to the man on the porch. "I grew up in Heart Falls, so I know all the secret back routes. There was an old gravel road about five feet from where the car landed. Once I got her hooked up, it was simple to pull her out." Brooke's gaze lifted past Ryan to meet Madison's. "Hey, there."

"Hi."

Ryan backed up to let the other couple pass. "Come in, and I'll introduce you properly."

Both Brooke and Mack examined Madison sharply as they left their shoes at the door and stepped into the front foyer.

"Oh, right. My face. The airbag," Madison offered as an explanation.

Understanding dawned on Brooke's face. "Which reminds me. Since the air bag was deployed, I have to bring the vechicle to the shop. It's not legal for you to drive her over."

Mack actually stepped forward, leaning a little closer as he eyed her carefully. "Looks as if you got off lucky. And *unlucky,* to have the air bag trigger. You couldn't have been moving very fast by that point on the hill unless you were really gunning it on the highway. And I doubt that, considering the road conditions."

Ryan put a hand to Mack's shoulder and pushed him aside. "I already gave her a physical, so stop hovering."

"Sorry, occupational hazard," Mack returned easily, holding out a hand to Madison. "Mack Klassen. Canadian Air Force, retired, and now with the Heart Falls fire department."

As Madison accepted the handshake, she didn't bother to hide her smile. "Ah. One of Ryan's. I'm not offended. I'm surprised you didn't try to casually check my pupils or take my pulse."

"Give him time," Brooke said, extending her own hand. "Brooke Klassen. And Mack is one of Ryan's, but he's mostly mine. We've been married since last March."

"Congratulations, a few months late," Madison said with a grin. She glanced down and decided what she was wearing would do.

Ryan misinterpreted her move. "Want me to grab your suitcase out of the car?"

"No problem, I can do it." She twisted toward the door.

Two male bodies blocked her way.

"Go. Sit," Ryan ordered. "Mack and I will grab your stuff while you and Brooke get acquainted."

"Testosterone has been activated. No use in arguing with them," Brooke assured her. "Come sit down so I can ask you what work you want done on your vehicle. I'll order in a replacement airbag to start, which will take at least a day."

Madison nodded at Brooke before turning to meet Ryan's eyes. "Don't bring everything. Just the suitcase in the back seat. Oh, and the box on the passenger seat labelled *Making Mischief*. That's all I need."

The two guys headed into the blustery weather. Madison was happy to remain in the warm house.

"I got myself a drink already," Brooke told her, striding into the living room.

Which meant Madison felt no guilt at returning to her previous spot on the couch. She grabbed the fuzzy blanket that had been draped over the back, spread it over her legs, then picked up her ginger ale. "Thank you for bringing my car."

"Seriously, it wasn't a problem. I'm glad you weren't hurt more. You must've pissed off the airbag sensors just enough when you left the road that they malfunctioned."

"I wondered what had happened. I mean it was bumpy, but I didn't slam into anything," Madison told her.

Brooke waved a hand. "Oh, I could tell from how the car was sitting that you did a good job hitting the ditch. No, sometimes airbags malfunction. I'm a mechanic, so if it hasn't happened to me personally, I've heard the story from someone."

The front door opened. The guys carried in her two items and headed into the guest room as they chatted easily.

Madison focused on Brooke. "When you install the new airbag, do you recommend any other tune-ups? I'll need to drive cross-country in a few weeks, so I want it to be roadworthy."

"I'll do an overall maintenance check," Brooke assured her. "And double-check the other airbags. But seriously, don't go thinking you did something wrong. I once had an airbag go off on me while I was in the middle of working under the dashboard. Damn thing hit me in the solar plexus so hard, I couldn't breathe. That was fun. Twisted half in, half out of the car, gasping for air like a fish out of water."

Mack and Ryan had rejoined them. "When was that?" Mack asked.

Brooke wrinkled her nose. "About three years ago. You should've seen the bruises."

"I think I will," Madison said dryly, but she winked. "So, tell me about Heart Falls. What do I need to do while I'm here?"

"That depends on where you're from," Brooke said dryly.

"Surrey," Mack and Ryan answered at the same time.

Brooke's husband grinned at Madison. "Hanging out at the fire hall involves lots of late nights and long conversations. Ryan's mentioned your name often."

"Every time I told him a high school story about getting in trouble. It was really tough to leave you out of it," Ryan admitted.

Madison pressed a hand to her chest. "Me? I'm sure you have me mistaken with some other hell-raising individual."

Brooke's eyes brightened as she smiled. "Oh. *You're* the one Ryan used to get detention with."

"There really is no use in denying it," Ryan said. "Although, Maddy is also the reason I survived calculus class. So, I should give credit where credit is due."

"That's neat that you guys go back that far," Brooke said.

"Best friends for a lot of years," Madison said contentedly. "Plus, I introduced him to Justina. I get credit for that one as well."

Ryan grinned. "You totally set us up."

Brooke sipped her drink, her gaze darting between Ryan and Madison in a way that said her mind was whirling. But instead of asking a personal question, Brooke gave an answer to the one Madison had originally asked. "You should do a tour of all the hotspots in town. My shop, the fire hall."

"Definitely the fire hall," Mack said quickly. "Tomorrow is teambuilding night. We've got a potluck dinner and movies—one for the kids and one for people who don't want to watch *Frozen* for the twelve-millionth time."

"*Some* people are missing their funny bone," Brooke teased. "You still don't know all the words."

Mack glared.

"Seriously, you need to *let it go…*"

He tickled her.

She wiggled away, fighting to keep from spilling her drink. "Stop." Brooke put the glass down and then turned back to Madison. "Other places include coffee at Buns and Roses, a trip to Fallen Books—that's our specialty indie store in town. The animal shelter is fun to visit, if you're at all interested in dogs, cats, and other critters."

"If you want to go for a horse ride, we've got a bunch of different options we can arrange," Ryan suggested. "Oh, and you know, if you feel like it, I suppose I could take you to Rough Cut."

"A bar? That's a bit on the wild side, isn't it?" Madison grinned at him. "Honestly? I can't wait to see the place."

~

Sitting with his friends, with Madison there, talking about the fun activities they should enjoy while she was around, somehow made December feel a lot more festive than it had earlier in the day.

Ryan had to admit—something was off this year. Even Talia seemed reluctant to get into the holiday spirit.

He'd pulled out the decorations a few days ago, and usually that would have triggered his daughter to dive in and demand they put everything up immediately.

She'd barely glanced at them this go-round.

Now that Madison was here, though, he could change that. Once Talia was home tomorrow, they could all put their heads together and come up with ideas on how to make the holidays extra special, including planning Talia's birthday party.

Also to talk about—his friends' arrival had cut short the discussion about what exactly Madison wanted to *fix*. The two of them needed to come back to that. Her meddling was always interesting, to say the least.

He'd never yet known her to be wrong about what she wanted to meddle in, though...

Ryan pulled his attention back to the conversation at hand. "We'll be at the pub Thursday afternoon and Friday night for a live crowd."

"We're still putting together Christmas hampers on Saturday afternoon?" Brooke asked.

"Yes," Ryan confirmed. "You two still on to help?"

"Of course." Mack nodded then leaned forward, concern on his rugged face. "Did you manage to get all the supplies lined up?"

A moment of unease slid in, but Ryan was able to answer honestly. "We'll be okay for Saturday. It's been a bad year for donations, though. Putting together the hampers and a few gift cards for the families who need them is pretty much going to leave the Heart Falls Hope Fund depleted."

"We need another fundraiser," Brooke said slowly.

Ryan nodded. "Terrible time of year for it." He glanced at Madison. "That food bank thing we took over. Last year, my co-coordinator and I dealt with the legwork but nothing on the financial end. This year, the old coordinators handed everything to us in October, and there wasn't nearly enough in the fund to last the entire winter."

"That's rough," Madison said. "December isn't an easy time of year to get people to open their wallets."

Mack asked a question about something else, and the conversation drifted for a while. Brooke shared a story about finding a field mouse colony in the back seat of an SUV. Mack told them about the time a skunk wandered into the fire hall. It was comfortable and easy.

Until Madison yawned.

She covered it quickly, but both Brooke and Mack offered grins as they got to their feet.

"We'll have more time to visit in the coming days," Brooke said. "We should've realized you'd be tired from the long drive and the excitement."

"It was really good to meet you," Madison said. "I'm looking forward to the time I get to spend here in Heart Falls."

"Get some sleep," Mack ordered, once again checking out her bruised face. He glanced at Ryan. "You need anything, give me a shout."

"She'll be fine, but thanks," Ryan said sincerely as he walked his friends to the door.

Madison went with them, yet she was all but swaying once they'd driven away.

He shook his head as he caught her by the shoulders and marched her toward the guest room. "You'd think by now you would've learned how to say *I'm tired*."

"But I was having fun," Madison insisted, resting her head on his shoulder as they walked slowly. "Bed will feel good."

He squeezed the arm around her shoulders then let her go. She gave him a little finger wave before the door closed between them.

It was definitely not the night off he'd expected. None of it.

It wasn't quite ten, so Ryan went and made himself a cup of tea then sat in his chair and twisted to stare out the window at the snow that was now falling straight down in huge, fluffy flakes.

What a night.

It had started with him restless enough to spend time pondering in the cemetery. Solar-powered lights hung from miniature shepherd hooks scattered between the old gravestones and the new. He'd walked for a while, cleaning up as he paced, letting his racing thoughts calm.

It'd been the kind of mental-rambling night that made him even more aware of missing Justina's company. The company of another adult to share things that he couldn't talk about with Talia. Things that would be good to talk about, but not with Mack or Alex or Brad at the fire hall.

Things he wanted to talk about with a woman.

Also, time he wanted to spend with a woman *not* talking. Definitely not talking.

To have Madison show up out of the blue was a bit of a miracle. An early Christmas present, at least in terms of having someone to talk to.

The physical part that he was now willing to admit he craved would have to be answered after his friend had left. It had never been sexual between them. Not that he didn't find Madison attractive, but she'd been his best friend. No way was he screwing that up by hitting on her. And Madison seemed to have felt the same way. She truly had been the one to set him up with Justina.

Ryan finished his tea then headed to bed.

He woke surprisingly late to the scent of coffee and buttered toast.

In the kitchen, he found Madison perched on one of the barstools at the island, legs curled under her.

She'd pulled a blue-and-red checked flannel shirt over a pale-blue top. White-washed jeans that fit her very nicely covered her thighs, but it was the bright-orange socks poking out from under her that made Ryan grin the hardest.

"Are those hazard indicators, Maddy?"

She glanced up from the paper she was reading. "Hey. Did I wake you?"

He shook his head as he stepped closer, tucking his fingers under her chin and lifting her face so he could examine her eyes closer. "I slept really solid. Your bruises aren't too bad."

"They feel okay as well." She lifted her cup and pointed

toward the counter. "I made a full pot of coffee. I didn't know what your schedule is for today. We never got to finish that conversation, but I did see pickup time on the fridge for Talia at nine a.m."

Which gave them an hour. They used it to make the rest of breakfast together and talk about the day ahead.

Including Ryan's somewhat failed attempts to make it clear he didn't expect her to do anything while she visited. "You're welcome to hang out here at the house and relax as much as you want. Or if you need information about places to go for shopping or anything else, we're only a couple of hours away from Calgary."

"I didn't come to go shopping," Madison said, shaking her head. "I came to see *you*. Besides, I just came from a big city—I'm not looking for bright lights. I want to help however I can. Maybe I can figure out a fundraiser to help with your Hope Fund problem."

Ryan checked his watch. "Well, for now, you can come help pick up Talia."

Madison was enthralled the entire drive up to Lone Pine ranch where Ryan's friend Brad and his wife, Hanna, were raising their family. Maddy peered out the window, whistling softly as the ranch house came into view at the top of the long driveway. It was a pretty bungalow with a neat barn beside it. Half a dozen horses wandered in the arena.

The inch of fresh snow that had fallen last night made everything white and bright, and warm, yellow lights glowed out of the windows.

"It's kind of like a Christmas card, isn't it?" Madison asked as she glanced toward him.

"Brad's family has lived here for years. He's a good guy, and you'll love his wife." Ryan stopped to the side of the house, glancing over at her as she pushed the door unsuccessfully. "Hang on. It sticks sometimes. I'll let you out."

She was still peering up at the house as he came around and opened her door with a sharp tug. She accepted his hand, but as her feet hit the ground, he was close enough to hear her soft grunt of pain.

He held on to her a second longer until she looked up. "You okay?"

Madison shrugged. "I'm fine. Just twigged one of the bruises over my rib cage."

Dammit. He felt like a shit for not having thought about this sooner. "When we get home, I'll find that cream for you."

Even before Ryan hit the doorbell, the sound of little-girl laughter drifted from the happy home.

A moment later the door opened to reveal Hanna, a petite, dark-haired woman, her baby boy balanced on her hip. She wore an astonishingly peaceful expression considering the volume of noise behind her.

She smiled at Ryan then glanced at Madison, frowning slightly. "Hi, Ryan. Talia is almost ready."

Ryan gestured toward his friend. "Hanna, this is Madison. We go way back. She's come for a visit." He twisted to Madison. "Hanna Ford. And the little tyke is Drew."

"Nice to meet you, Hanna." Madison cleared her throat. "And just in case you were worried, the dark eyes are because of a slight vehicle incident. I'm okay."

Hanna examined her for another moment then dipped her chin. "Good to know."

In the hallway just past the mudroom, Ryan could see his daughter, plus Hanna's dark-haired Crissy, and a third little girl, Emma Stone, her blonde curls bouncing as she moved.

Crissy, Emma and Talia were all taking turns doing pirouettes, two with arms outstretched around the one in the middle as she twirled. It seemed like a good idea to have two spotters for one dancer, because none of them were keeping their feet very well.

Hanna shifted the baby from one hip to the other. "They have been buzzing all night, completely obsessed with this ballet performance the teacher hopes to pull together."

Ryan thought back, worried he'd missed something during pickup from lessons on Monday night. "I don't remember a performance being on the calendar."

Hanna waved a hand. "There isn't one. Not really, and if it does happen, it's not going to be anything big. Charity started making calls to each of us individually last night to find out how much energy we could commit. Talia *Zhao* means you're probably last on the list." Hanna glanced back at Crissy then down at six-month-old Drew. "I want her to have the fun, but I really can't promise to spend too much extra time. Not right now."

"Maybe that's something I could help with," Madison offered. She twisted toward Ryan. "Up to you, definitely, and only if it works after I talk to the dance teacher."

"You're here to have a holiday," Ryan protested.

Madison's brow rose. "If I'm going to hang around, I may as well do something productive. Also, you mentioned needing a fundraiser. I should come up with an idea that would make the girls happy *and* put some money in the pot."

Ryan twisted toward her. "Why am I suddenly scared?"

"Because you have far too vivid an imagination," Madison suggested, winking at Hanna. "Don't worry. I'm not that dangerous."

"A little danger is sometimes good," Hanna said softly. "Call me if you need help. I don't know how much hands-on I can provide, but brainstorming, I can manage."

Then Talia was there, pulling on her coat and giving her friends farewell hugs. A moment later Ryan helped buckle her into the booster seat in the back of the crew cab truck—his daughter was still short enough she needed a lift so that the seat belt worked properly—while Talia talked a mile a minute about everything she'd done during the sleepover. "...and I really like the kittens. I think we should get one, Daddy."

"Take a breath, little one. I want you to say hi to my friend Madison."

Talia froze. She leaned to the side and peered up with great interest at the strange woman beside him. "Hi. Your eyes are purple."

4

The past couple of minutes had been such a whirlwind. Madison was thoroughly enjoying herself, though, including examining Ryan's daughter with a touch of nostalgia.

Talia was a pretty little thing, with long black hair currently pulled into a slightly lopsided ponytail. Her big, dark eyes and the straight line of her nose were Ryan, but her lips and chin were identical to her mother's. Justina had been a pixie, with lips that were always slightly pursed as if waiting for a kiss.

Madison leaned on the door and offered Talia her hand. "I do have purple eyes right now. Would you like to shake hands to say hello?"

Talia blinked and then grinned, catching hold of Madison's fingers. She held on firmly and gave a couple of quick shakes before letting go, her gaze still drifting over Madison's face. "Daddy taught me how."

"That was a very polite handshake," Ryan assured her. "You girls okay if we head home? Talia still has school this afternoon, so we should go get ready."

"I got to have a sleepover last night even though it was a

school night." Talia started talking again the instant Madison had gotten into the front seat and done up her seat belt. "That doesn't happen very often. The teachers had a special event this morning, so we don't have to go to school until after lunch. Crissy asked if Emma and I could come for a sleepover, and Mrs. Ford said we could."

Madison twisted enough to put an arm on the back of the seat and semi-face Talia. "That sounds as if it was a treat."

"We had so much fun. Only her baby brother cries sometimes, and he woke me up." Talia made a face. "Emma said her baby brother cries, too. I don't think I want to have a baby brother."

Ryan coughed lightly, keeping his focus on the road ahead. "That's good to know."

"Do you work with my daddy?" Talia asked. "Because I know he works with Grace. And he works with Charity. And he works with Rose."

Madison glanced at Ryan, keeping her amusement off her face as best she could. "Sounds as if your daddy has lots of friends."

He gave her a moment of side eye, and she grinned.

"Daddy does have lots of friends," Talia agreed. "How come I haven't met you before?"

"But you have," Madison told her. "You were a lot littler the last time I saw you. And you were *very* little the first time I saw you, which was a couple of days after you were born."

Talia's eyes went even wider, and her jaw dropped slightly in surprise. "You saw me when I was a baby?"

"I did. I even brought some of those pictures with me. I can show them to you when we have more time." Madison watched as the little girl leaned back in the seat and considered this shocking news.

And then the smart little thing put two and two together. "That means you knew my mommy."

That pulse of sadness arrived, the one that always struck when Madison thought about the tragedy of losing Justina so young. "I knew your mommy very well. She and I were friends, just like your daddy and I were friends."

It seemed to take a little longer for Talia to process this, and she fell silent until they were pulling into the driveway outside the house.

They were all out of the truck, headed for the front door, when Talia paused. "How did you get here?"

"I drove."

Talia glanced down the street before running to the garage and peering in. She turned back with a frown. "Where's your car?"

"At the shop. It needed some repairs."

"Oh." Talia considered this. "Is it a big car?"

"Big enough. I have my bicycle and my clothes and books and some kitchen stuff with me."

Talia's eyes widened. "Why?"

"I'm moving," Madison told her. "I had to bring what I would need in the new place I'll live."

Talia ran ahead and darted in the door Ryan had opened, taking off her boots and hanging up her coat at the hook by the entrance, but when she turned around, she was frowning. "How come you have to move?"

"Because I have a new job in a different city, so that means I can't live with my family anymore."

"How come—?"

Ryan interrupted her. "Talia, I know Madison doesn't mind playing twenty questions, but *you* need to get a couple things done this morning. And we need to go pick up some groceries."

Madison thought quickly. She waited until Talia was busy at the kitchen table with what was obviously her school backpack then spoke softly to Ryan so that she wasn't overruling or causing trouble with her suggestion. "Do you need Talia to come with you to do the groceries, or can I stay here and supervise her while you shop on your own?"

For a moment he looked as if he would protest. Probably about to say something about how she was there to relax and not babysit.

"I wouldn't have offered if I weren't serious," Madison added quickly. "Only if she's okay with the idea, of course."

But when the question was put to her, Ryan speaking quietly beside the kitchen table, Talia seemed greatly excited by the idea. "I can help you unpack. Daddy says you're staying for the holidays."

"Your daddy is a bossy pants," Madison said without thinking, causing Talia to burst into a fit of childish giggles.

"Yes, yes, I am," Ryan said in a very distinguished and serious tone of voice. "And now I am going to go *bossy pants* all the groceries we need into a cart and all the way home. Any requests, Maddy?"

"I'm easy, but I do love anything chocolate."

Talia stood beside her, nodding vigorously. "Me too."

Ryan made sure that Madison had his current cell number, then he disappeared, leaving her with his daughter.

Like her mother so many years earlier, Talia was not shy. She grabbed Madison by the hand and all but tugged her toward the guest room. "My friend Chrissy has people stay at their house all the time. And Emma, too, although it's usually her Uncle Dustin, or her grandpa, or one of her second-removed cousins. Emma's mommy explained what that meant, but I think it's a funny word that means you have too much family."

The second-removed thing was hysterical. Madison got such a kick out of kids and their honest, outspoken truths.

But the other part of Talia's comment was the more important bit right now. It explained why the idea of somebody staying with them was a lot more exciting than Madison had expected.

She was glad. She wouldn't have wanted to make Ryan's daughter uncomfortable.

"It can be very fun to have visitors," Madison agreed. "I'm looking forward to spending time with you, but you have to let me know if you need time alone. That's part of being a good guest."

Talia climbed on the foot of the guest bed—a queen-size mattress—and looked expectantly around the room. Her gaze fell on the single suitcase and lone box, and for a moment she looked disappointed. "Do you want me to get some more things from your car?"

"This is enough. The first thing we should do is unpack that."

Talia bounced to her feet and over to the cardboard box Madison had pointed at. She peered at it before dragging a finger over the letters Madison had drawn on in bold Sharpie.

"Making Mischief." Talia glanced at Madison. "What does that mean?"

"It means every time I find something that would make a good present for someone I know, I put it in the box. And usually by the time the holidays come around, or someone's birthday, I have just what I need already tucked away."

This little girl had such an expressive face. She seemed to think Madison's gift box was the most amazing idea ever. "This is full of *presents*?"

"A little less full now than it was before. I took out the things I had bought for my two brothers and my mom before I left home. But there are some things in there for Christmas here in Heart Falls. But before presents, I need help to hide something for your daddy."

For the first time, Talia eyed her with something less than approval. "Secrets?"

Madison considered for a moment then shook her head. "Not really a secret. A surprise. See, when your dad and I were friends at school, we had a tradition that always made us happy."

She reached past Talia and loosened off the lid of the box. The topmost item sat there in all its sparkly glory. Madison lifted it out carefully then laid it on the bed.

Talia was speechless. Then she got a little giggly, briefly covering her mouth with her hands. "That's for *Daddy*?"

"Sort of. He gets to have it for a little while. That's part of the fun tradition." Madison spread the red, bedazzled sweater out a little more, grinning at Talia. "*This* is an ugly sweater."

"It's very ugly," Talia agreed, "but I like the sparkles."

"It's ugly *and* it sparkles, which makes it perfect," Madison told her. "So, here's how the tradition works. Once we find the sweater, we have to wear it. And not just at home, but out in public where other people will see. Then we hide it all over again so the other person will unexpectedly find it, and so on."

Talia was giggling again. "I can help you hide it."

"Somewhere your daddy won't find until tomorrow morning." Ryan had said there was an event at the fire hall tonight, and Madison probably shouldn't be mean to him right off the bat.

Her co-conspirator seemed to know the exactly right spot because her eyes widened, and her mouth formed an excited O. "I know."

She took off like a shot. Madison followed, not eager to infringe on Ryan's privacy but needing to ensure Talia wasn't doing anything like climbing a bookcase to get to the hiding place.

Once the sweater was successfully hidden, Madison curled her finger, motioning for Talia to join her. "Now we have to pretend we didn't do that and not tell your daddy anything about it so it's a surprise. Want to help me with the rest of my things? Then I can get out the photo album."

Talia dashed across the room, catching Madison by the hand and pulling her back to her room. "You should show us pictures when Daddy is home. He'll want to see them, too."

For the next half hour, Madison pulled things from her suitcase and let Talia stick them in whichever drawer she wanted. Then Talia arranged the small amount of makeup and personal items Madison had on the counter in the bathroom.

By this time, they were ready to deal with the school things Talia needed to wrangle, but all in all, Madison felt as if it had been a wonderful morning.

She couldn't wait to see Ryan's face when he discovered the sweater.

RYAN PULLED BACK into his own driveway and paused, eyeing the holiday wreath hanging on his front door. A big, gaudy thing with enormous golden bells and a thick, red velvet ribbon poking outward in giant loopy loops.

Madison had found the decorations. But not *his* decorations, because he sure didn't remember ever having bought a monstrosity like that.

"Daddy," Talia shouted as he walked in the door with the first load of groceries. "Madison is making grilled cheese for lunch."

"Yum," Ryan announced as expected. "Come help me bring things in and put them away."

The familiar task turned slightly awkward because they had an audience. Madison was busy at the counter beside the stove, which meant she was out of the way for the most part. It wasn't until he brushed past her for the third time that Ryan realized how tight the work triangle was in his kitchen.

But Talia continued to chatter. Madison answered when she had to but otherwise just made humming noises when appropriate. Ryan slid past her again to get to the cupboard where he kept the coffee, keenly aware of the lack of distance between them.

Bumping into her soft curves—

Madison laughed at something Talia said, and Ryan pulled himself together. Obviously, it'd been too long since he'd had another adult in his house. That was all.

"Did you get everything you needed?" Madison asked as they sat down to the grilled cheese and tomato soup she'd pulled together.

"I did, including a couple of things you might like."

"Chocolate," Talia guessed excitedly.

"Some," Ryan said with a nod. "Did you have a good morning?"

Talia glanced up at Madison, her little face a bright, open book. "Madison has some pretty clothes. They make me think of sunshine."

Ryan glanced at the neon-orange socks on his friend's feet. "Maddy likes to brighten up people's days."

The final hour before having to drop Talia at school passed in a blur. Madison offered to stay at home, but Talia had other ideas.

"You have to see where I go to school. And you need to meet my teacher," his little girl insisted.

Madison checked with Ryan before agreeing. "Just remember I told you if you need space, I can visit quietly somewhere else for a little bit. Having guests can be fun, but sometimes we need a break."

"I know," Talia said.

Ryan wasn't quite sure what his daughter was up to. He attempted to offer a warning, but Madison waved it off. "I have an idea what's going on. I'll tell you later, but this is fine."

He was glad one of them knew what was up, because when they hit the schoolyard, Talia dragged Madison forward to where a whole bevy of little girls waited.

Madison focused intently on each one, solemnly offering handshakes or high fives depending on what they wanted.

A firm grip landed on his shoulder, and Ryan twisted to see his friend Brad Ford, Hanna's husband and the local fire chief, grinning at him. The man's shaved head contrasted with the neatly trimmed beard he was growing.

"That your visitor?" Brad asked

"Maddy? Yeah. Good friend from a lot of years ago." Ryan glanced over, but Madison was now leaning down and listening intently to some story being told by one of Talia's cohorts. "Hanna met her this morning."

"Hanna liked her. Said she seems pretty down to earth." Brad straightened and wiggled his fingers at Crissy, who was waving frantically.

Ryan snorted as suddenly the entire group of little girls waved wildly in their direction. Madison grinned then lifted one hand and did the royal wave while blinking madly. "Maybe this isn't a great idea. Madison is going to teach them so many dangerous things."

"Yeah, I somehow doubt that." Brad took a step back then gave a quick head nod. "I should go. But I'll see you tonight at the hall."

"We'll be there," Ryan promised.

It wasn't until the school bell went off that Madison managed to free herself from the clutches of the grade four class.

She laughed as they got back into the truck. "Your daughter is a hoot," she informed him. Her bright smile grew slightly more serious. "Thank you so much for giving me a chance to get to know her better. And to spend time with you. I think this is exactly what I needed."

"You had a dire need to come and do somebody else's chores for a month?" Ryan focused on the road, but he wasn't going to let her get away without ponying up some information today. "Before I drive too far, you want to go anywhere in town first?"

"What's on your agenda?" Madison asked. "And before you say whatever I want, remember the whole *this is your life and I'm invading it* point? What do you usually do after dropping Talia off at school on a Wednesday?"

"Usually I'd have just come off a night shift at seven a.m., so I'd be headed home to sleep. And I'd have another twelve-hour shift on Wednesday night, starting at seven p.m. until seven, but this week is out of whack. Between Talia's short school day and tonight's team-building event at the fire hall, my friend Alex took last night, and Mack is on duty tonight."

"That was nice of them."

Ryan nodded. "It was. Alex and Mack are both rock-solid. Plus, Mack has already warned me that at some point, he and Brooke will be having kids, and then he'll expect to be given a break."

Madison nodded slowly. "Let's head back to your place, and we can talk about what the next few weeks will look like. But it's pretty neat you've got that kind of work setup with your friends. I'm glad."

"Me too."

When they got home, he pointed at the gaudy wreath hanging off his front door. Didn't say anything, just raised a brow.

She grinned. "I'm only responsible for half of it," she said quickly. "Talia chose the ribbon."

"Of course, she did," Ryan said, resisting the urge to roll his eyes. "Thank you for my decoration."

"You're welcome," Madison said cheerfully, grinning as she paced past him into the house.

This time, he didn't bother to fight, simply dropped his calendar on the table and went through it with her. "It takes a little juggling, but I get Talia to and from school every day, and even though I'm not here every night, I almost always get to phone to say good night."

"Talia is not hurting one bit," Madison assured him. "She loves you to pieces, and she knows exactly how important she is to you. I know this because she told me, a number of times."

Ryan couldn't stop a grin. "Really?"

"Really." Madison leaned back in her chair. "I think your schedule is going to exhaust me, but I'm game to try."

He laughed. "Mad, You don't have to come to work with me."

"Oh, I am totally not doing your twelve-hour shifts," she assured him. "But what I am going to do is deal with a few little things that have kind of flown under your radar."

"For example?" He hated to ask, but once Madison got her mind set on something, it would be hard to make her change tracks. Better he knew now what she was plotting.

"Unless you absolutely hate the idea, or have some other reason why you're holding off, you want me to deal with getting you a big-boy bed?" She said it quietly then waited as if gauging his response.

"My bed offends you that much?" If this was the worst thing she wanted to fix, he had no problem accepting her help.

She shrugged. "I'm not offended, but again, unless you have a reason why you want things to stay the way they are, I'll put together a couple of options, and then all you have to do is approve one. And pay for it, of course."

Ryan could see zero downfall to this bit of interference. "Have at her."

Madison grinned. "Thank you. Second thing. You want me to make a list of potential women for you to date? Because I set you up once. I can probably do it again."

5

Ryan's ears grew hot, possibly because her words whirled so rapidly, his brain was overheating. "You want to set me up?"

"Well, you said you're considering getting back into the dating scene. I've seen your schedule, dude." She pointed at the calendar notes spread on the table. "The right woman could walk under your nose, but unless she's on fire, there's a good chance you won't even notice."

Amusement snuck in hard. "I acknowledge you set me up the first time, but Justina was one in a million."

Madison dipped her chin. "Agreed. Which is why you need a list of options, because frankly, it sounds as if you might have a problem in this area."

Indignation rose. Ryan folded his arms over his chest. "A problem in *what* area exactly?"

She snorted then wiped a hand over her mouth. "Excuse me. Not *that* way, jeez. You're such a guy. All touchy when you think your sexual prowess has been insulted."

Ryan was outright laughing now. "This list is getting more and more curious."

"I just think, with how much you have on your plate, you should let somebody you trust who has a new perspective on the world around you offer some suggestions." Madison said it as if she were a lawyer presenting detailed instructions to the most serious jury out there.

Ryan pressed his palms to the table and leaned forward, meeting her gaze intently. "You crack me up."

She matched him, position for position. "Just call me Yenta."

He paused. Considered. "That's got to be from one of your old movies, but hell if I know which one."

She sat back and waved a hand in the air. "Oh, my young apprentice. So soon you have forgotten the lessons of the classics. From *Fiddler on the Roof*. Yenta was a matchmaker, which is what I'll be for you, only I'm less bossy, and you don't have to pay me in chickens."

Dear God. "That's good, because I'm severely short on chickens at the moment. I couldn't figure out how to fold them to put them in my wallet."

Madison laughed out loud— a bright, happy sound—as she rubbed her hands together. "But now for the really important thing that I'd like to do. Do you mind if I contact Talia's dance teacher and see what she's got in mind? Because, face it, I have more spare time than you at the current moment."

Having something special in dancing for Talia to look forward to—how on earth could Ryan turn down that offer? "Let me give Charity a shout and see what she's got in mind. She's also a volunteer with the firefighting crew, so you'll see her tonight."

"A firefighting ballerina—there's a sight you don't see very often." Madison made a few notes on the paper in front of her.

Ryan made his phone call while Madison pulled out her laptop and hooked up to his Wi-Fi. The afternoon passed quickly, and they were heading out the door to pick up Talia when Ryan swore softly.

"I totally forgot I was supposed to make something." He glanced at Madison. "It's a potluck tonight."

Madison stepped back. "Go. This is exactly why I'm here. Grab Talia, and I'll rampage through your cupboards and figure out something to bring."

"We can stop at the deli and grab something," Ryan suggested.

"Already have an idea," Madison assured him. "Go, grab your kiddo."

There was no use in arguing. Ryan hurried over to the school, joining a group of other parents by the schoolyard fence as he waited for his daughter to appear.

Talia came racing up to the dismissal gate, peering past him eagerly. "Where's Madison?"

"Getting ready for tonight. Come on, we need to get ready as well."

Talia looked totally disappointed, shoulders drooping as she twisted toward where the school buses were lined up. She shouted across the snowy yard. "She's not here."

Little Emma Stone made a sad face before waving and joining her sister on the bus.

Ryan kept his amusement to himself until Talia was buckled up in her booster seat and they were on their way home. "Did you have a good afternoon at school?"

"I had a math test that was super easy. And Emma and I made snowmen at recess, only Darren and Josh knocked them over." Talia reached forward and grabbed the back of the car's seat in front of her. "Is Madison really staying with us for the holidays?"

"She really is. Is that okay with you?"

"*Yes*," Talia all but shouted.

Ryan eyed her in the rearview mirror. Talia was excitable at the best of times, but now she seemed to be nearly vibrating.

It had to be them having a houseguest for the first time in a long time. Madison had mentioned Talia sharing how all her friends had people stay over on a regular basis.

He needed to make sure to bring his parents out to Heart Falls a little more often in the new year. Of course, that could complicate his future dating life even more… Once he managed to start *having* a dating life.

Dear God, Madison was making him a list of potential girlfriends. He didn't know if he should laugh or start running.

Talia vanished into the house to get ready for the evening's gathering. Ryan went to grab a shovel to clean the walkways before they left, stuttering to a stop as he realized they were already clear.

Madison had struck again.

Inside the house, he found her tidying up at the sink. She placed a mixing bowl into the drying rack as she glanced over her shoulder at him. "Hey. The tornado that is Talia just informed me that she'll be out in a few minutes. I've got our potluck contribution ready, and I'm dressed."

Ryan nodded as he glanced over her quickly. She still wore those faded white jeans and the neon-orange socks, but she'd exchanged her shirt for a soft green sweater with a row of pearl buttons down the front. It was slightly festive, a little dressy, but perfect for a small-town community event.

She'd also applied makeup, and the faint black shadows from the accident were no longer instantly apparent. In fact, her cheeks were rosy, and her eyes looked even brighter than usual. The red highlights in her hair seemed brighter than before, the soft length falling around her shoulders.

He dragged his gaze off the shiny red on her lips. "It won't take me long, either. We'll still be plenty early."

She waved him off, and Ryan headed to the master bedroom. He grabbed a quick shower, reconsidering what to wear that night. A plain old T-shirt wasn't quite dressy enough to match Madison's outfit, and he didn't want her to feel uncomfortable.

When he reached for his towel, it wasn't there on the towel bar. He didn't remember tossing it in the hamper, but he must've. No way around it. He stepped onto the bathmat, dripped his way across to the linen closet, jerking it open to pull out—

Directly in front of him lay a memory. The red cardigan was in pristine shape, and still as god-awful as he remembered. "Madison, you are one hundred percent mischief," he muttered under his breath as he reached past the sweater for a towel.

He stared at the monstrosity as he rubbed rapidly at his hair and body then grabbed it out and made his way into the bedroom.

Spreading the sweater on the bed just made it clearer exactly how hideous the thing was. Still, Ryan found himself grinning from ear to ear and unable to stop.

Once upon a time, the sweater had been a simple red plaid. Black vertical lines and systematic chevrons divided it into a grid pattern, and he supposed it would've been rather sharp paired with black jeans. Only, at some point, the Christmas elves—aka Madison—had got their fingers on the cardigan, and now extra pockets were plastered everywhere. Christmas-themed decals were artistically strewn over its surface. Not to mention the gold and silver buttons, tiny lights, green beads, and the occasional tuft of silver thread as if someone had tossed tinsel into the knitting machine in a frenzy.

While he admired—*ha*—the sweater, he pulled on the rest of his clothes. Black jeans and a black T-shirt, because of course he was going to wear the *thing*.

It was tradition, and no way was he breaking that rule.

He took a quick hop back into the bathroom so he could

comb his hair. A single glance in the mirror was enough to set him shaking his head. It wasn't that the sweater looked *bad*, per se, but he was definitely making a statement. His friends were going to get an absolute kick out of it.

Ryan wondered how long he could keep a straight face and pretend he wasn't wearing anything out of the ordinary.

Stepping into the living room, Talia's nonstop prattling about dance moves turned into a shriek. "*Daddy*."

Madison somehow managed to look guilty and very amused at the same time. "I didn't know we were supposed to dress up," she said innocently.

Ryan shook a finger at her. "You fired the first shot. Just saying." He turned to his daughter and pivoted as he showed off his outfit. "So? What do you think?"

Her girlish giggle was sweet to his ears. "You look happy," Talia said. She moved forward and lowered her voice. "I helped hide it. Is that okay?"

"Of course," he reassured her. "Dressing in an ugly sweater is something fun. My friends Brooke and Mack did it last year. And I'll have you know this sweater is not just ugly, it's lucky."

Talia's eyes grew big. "Really?"

He nodded. "I was wearing this sweater when I met your mother," he informed her.

Talia glanced back at Madison. "That's *wild*."

Laughter burst free from Madison as she nodded her agreement. "That's very wild. Now we should probably go," she said, tapping her watch.

THEY WEREN'T the first to arrive at the fire hall, which meant voices and laughter and the sound of music greeted them as they walked in the front door on the main floor.

Talia vanished almost immediately, joining a group of

children gathered in the open space beside the fire engine, playing with skipping ropes and balls and other toys in haphazard piles. Madison recognized Crissy in the group.

Ryan motioned toward the young people. "Charity is with them. If you want to say hi."

"Sounds like a great idea." Madison had been pondering the entire time she'd put together the salad for the potluck. Inspiration was just waiting to be triggered. Hopefully talking to Talia's dance teacher would be what she needed.

They'd just arrived beside the young woman when Talia noticed, dropping her skipping rope and hauling Crissy with her. "See? Madison came." Talia tugged on Charity's hand. "This is my daddy's friend, Madison Joy."

Charity turned, a smile on her face as she glanced at Ryan and then Madison. In her early twenties, the woman had burnished brown skin and natural black curls that bounced around her face. "Hi, Madison. Nice to meet you."

"You too." Madison leaned past her slightly and whispered to the girls. "I've never met a ballerina before."

Her cheeks glowing, Charity was about to respond when a gasp escaped instead. "Oh, my."

Madison glanced beside her. Ryan had taken off his winter coat and now wore a very innocent expression as Charity gaped at the monstrosity covering his torso.

He twisted to Madison. "Give me your coat, and I'll hang them up. I should go make sure things are all set up, so pop upstairs when you're done."

"No problem," Madison said smoothly, turning back to Charity, who was opening and closing her mouth without any sound coming out. "I have a question for you about the dance thing you mentioned to Hanna."

Charity coughed into her elbow for a second, straightening with an enormous grin. "Sure, but first? Tell me you're responsible for that."

She jerked a thumb toward Ryan's retreating back.

Madison shrugged. "Highly unlikely. I mean, we're friends, but Ryan is pretty much responsible for himself."

The ballerina/firefighter snickered. "Okay. I'll be sure to give him all the grief when appropriate. Now, what do you want to know?"

It took a couple of minutes, then a couple of more because the children kept interrupting, wanting Charity and Madison to demonstrate that *they* knew how to skip and throw balls just as well as the preteens.

In the end, though, Madison had the beginnings of an idea for mischief that would not only make Talia and her friends happy but might help with Ryan's fundraiser issue as well.

Charity rubbed her hands together. "Let me write up a basic outline for you."

"We can talk later," Madison assured her.

"This won't take me too long. I'll touch base before you leave. I know we need to work pretty quick to make it happen."

As Madison stepped onto the second floor of the fire hall, the scent of sweet ham and something pumpkin-spiced filled her head.

She put the ambrosia salad she'd been carrying onto the long table with the rest of the food then glanced around in search of familiar faces.

She spotted Brooke first. The tall woman stood at the counter in the kitchen area talking to another dark-haired woman who was pulling a roasting pan from the oven.

Madison made her way over to join them.

Brooke smiled a greeting. "Hey. Good to see you." She gestured to the second woman who was transferring slices of ham to two different platters. "This is Yvette. I'd offer to take over for her, but with my luck, I'd manage to burn something."

"At least the fire trucks would be close by," Yvette teased.

She glanced over her shoulder at Madison. "Just a minute. I want to drizzle honey over them while they're hot."

"Yum." Madison glanced at Brooke. "That's quite a skill you've got if you can burn food while drizzling honey."

"Sweetheart, you have no idea." Brooke pressed the back of her hand against her forehead as if she were a damsel in distress. "Alas, I shall just have to perfect my cleanup skills and leave the cooking to others."

Yvette finished her task then wiped her hands on a towel, turning to greet Madison. "Welcome to Heart Falls."

"Thanks. Are you a firefighter?"

The other woman shook her head, ponytail bouncing. "Veterinarian. Brooke invited me."

"Bringing a friend along is the only way I survive these evenings," Brooke said softly. "Don't get me wrong. Firefighters are *wonderful*, but when they get talking shop? I mean, I know I can get pretty heated up about a new set of wrenches, but I don't tend to talk about my work nonstop."

"I guess this means I should stick with you two," Madison returned in the same quiet tone. "The only thing I know about fire is to douse it—"

Yvette's hand was over Madison's mouth a second later, Brooke tucking in front of her with a finger pressed sharply against her lips as she shook her head slightly from side to side. "*Shhh*."

Madison snickered but nodded her agreement.

Yvette's hand vanished. "Sorry about that, but I really didn't want you to have to listen to Firefighting 101 for the next hour."

Madison thought back to what she'd said. "What was the trigger word?"

"*Douse*," Brooke whispered. "Which implies you use water on everything, which is not true."

Fortunately, Madison realized what she was talking about. Water on an oil fire was not a good idea. "Smother?"

"Better. Extinguish is probably the safest." Yvette raised her voice to a normal level. "Well, I think we're ready for dinner. Ryan?"

It took a moment for Ryan to appear from the corner where he'd been talking to a couple of other guys. The instant he stepped forward, laughter bounced through the crowd as everyone who hadn't seen it yet spotted his sweater.

Brooke leaned against Madison's side. "Tell me you're responsible for that."

Too funny. "Why does everybody think I could get Ryan to do anything he didn't want?"

"Oh, you totally couldn't," Brooke agreed, but she was smiling widely. "That said, last year Ryan tricked Mack and I into wearing ugly sweaters on a night when nobody else was."

Madison pressed a hand against her chest. "No. I am shocked." Then she leaned forward. "Don't tell anyone, but that's kind of how the tradition with this sweater started. Plus, good things have come from it. Ryan met his wife while garbed like a drunken elf. I've had good things happen, too."

One of which she still needed to inform Ryan about, but considering she'd been around for less than forty-eight hours, they still had plenty of time to finish getting caught up.

Brooke guided her to the table, and Madison sat with the two women, looking around with curiosity. There was a wide mix of people at the event, from some young enough to be teenagers to a group of silver-haired gentlemen at the far end of the room.

Hanna joined them, little Drew carried off by Brad as he settled beside Ryan and Mack. They were joined by a man with light olive-brown skin who took off his cowboy hat before staring at Ryan.

"You'd think Alex had never seen an ugly sweater before," Brooke said dryly.

"It's such a very fine specimen," Hanna said, leaning back to take another look before shivering. "Wow. Anybody who wants to beat *that* has got to have some pretty awesome talent."

Yvette caught Madison glancing up and down the table as they ate. The next thing Madison knew, she was getting a quick rundown on the volunteer firefighting teams.

"Brad's full-time for the whole district. Mack's full-time here in Heart Falls, and we've got a couple of paid EMTs who just came on board this year." Yvette pointed across the table without actually pointing. "Ryan, Alex, and Ashton all head different volunteer crews."

"Alex and Ashton both work full time at Silver Stone ranch, but they each do about ten hours extra at the fire hall as well." Hanna added that tidbit.

Alex was the cowboy, and Ashton was one of the older gentlemen at the end of the table. And while ten hours of time was significant, it was less than the thirty Madison had calculated Ryan was doing. Still—

When he'd shared his schedule with her, his sense of pride that he'd managed to fit in all the things that were important to him had been clear.

That itchy feeling she got when something was just not quite right was back, though. She wasn't about to discuss her thoughts with the women. Until she knew what was off and how to fix it, she wasn't about to share with *anybody*, and even then—

She had already interfered in Ryan's life by showing up out of the blue. Plus, she'd threatened to make him buy a bed, and she was totally going to run with the dance and fundraiser idea. She was maybe sort of joking about the girlfriend list.

She wasn't about to butt in anymore unless it was crystal-clear it was the right thing to do.

Conversation drifted, relaxed and easy. Laughter rang from down the table as someone else complimented Ryan on his sweater.

Ryan rose to his feet then took a slight bow. "I am so disappointed in the rest of you. Such a missed opportunity."

Charity laughed. "Right. Because we were *all* supposed to wear something gaudy?"

"Why not?" Brad rose to his feet next to Ryan. "You just wanted to get a jump on it so you could win this year, but I'm telling you now. Next year? You're going to have some serious competition."

"Game on," Ryan said, brow raised.

"The Heart Falls Firefighters Annual Ugly Sweater Potluck." Alex considered. "I like it."

And just like that, Madison was present at the creation of a new annual event. She leaned back and caught Ryan's eye.

He winked, straightened his shoulders, and pretended to brush lint from his sleeves, although that just made the sparkling buttons flash even more.

The meal ended, and people split into different groups. Some tidied up, some got the kids set up with their movie.

Charity motioned her over. "Okay, here's what I've got."

The other woman held out a piece of paper that included a list of characters. Madison vaguely remembered the ballet, but in a way, that was good.

She glanced down the list. Names for "star" performers and what appeared to be five or six additional small groups. "And your dancers can perform in here? Because that's a key point."

"Definitely. They're not ready for the big time, but they've been practicing hard enough, it would be fun to get them up on stage," Charity assured her. "Right here."

She tapped one of the small groups. Madison nodded.

One part of the equation figured out, she thanked Charity then headed over to Ryan.

He was sitting with Alex, chatting easily. Ryan glanced up as she approached. "Having fun? I saw you were with Brooke and figured you'd be okay."

"Your friends are great, and I'm having a blast." Madison dropped into the chair beside him. She half listened to his easy conversation with the wiry cowboy while ideas for the potential fundraiser whirled in her brain.

The inspiration to create the monstrosity Ryan wore right now had come in the blink of an eye. She'd known from the start it would be something special and so much fun.

That same feeling of trembling on the edge of something magical teased her now.

She couldn't wait to see where inspiration finally landed.

Amusement rose. She couldn't wait to see Ryan jump through the hoops she created again, like usual, good-natured and energetic.

He glanced at her, paused his conversation, and sat bolt upright before announcing, "You're grinning."

"Am I?"

"You're sitting there, quietly, grinning from ear to ear." Ryan gave an exaggerated shudder, leaning closer to Alex and speaking in a mock whisper. "That expression she's wearing? That means we're in trouble."

"Well, that's promising." Alex rubbed his hands together. "A pretty lady wants to get me in trouble? I'm all for it." He winked then let out a sharp *ouch* as the elbow Ryan swung at him connected with his ribs.

Visions of sugar plums danced in her head.

6

Her second morning in Heart Falls, Madison offered to stay home while Ryan took Talia to school.

Talia was having none of it. She slid her fingers into Madison's, staring at her with a bit of a frown. "Don't you want to take me to school?"

Madison let her jaw drop. "Of course, I want to take you to school, but I don't want you to feel like you *have* to let me." She said the last part in a lower tone as if sharing a secret. "I'm going to be here for a while, and I don't want you to get bored of me."

"You're not boring," Talia informed her briskly. "Mr. Marche, our singing teacher, is boring. He makes us do scales before we get to sing, and he goes so low that the whole class sounds like cows. Doe, doe, doe, *doeeee*..."

She dropped the tone during the last part of that sentence. Madison laughed as she imagined an entire grade four class doing the same thing.

Once Talia was off to school, Madison looked at Ryan

eagerly. "If I remember your schedule correctly, you head to Rough Cut this afternoon."

He nodded. "I've got a bunch of deliveries coming in. And Grace will be there before we leave to grab Talia again, so I can introduce you."

"Okay. I want to get some work done this morning, but this afternoon, I'm all yours," Madison told him happily.

Ryan had work of his own, which suited her fine.

It took about an hour, but she figured out exactly what she needed to complete her first task right before lunch. When Ryan knocked on the door of her guest room, she had just finished stapling three packages together for him.

"I thought we could grab Subway on the way to the pub," Ryan offered.

"Sounds great."

Which meant when they slid in the back door of Ryan's pub, Madison was fully focused on enjoying herself.

"I should have taken you in the front way," he teased. "Let you feel the proper ambience."

"We'll do that next time," Madison suggested. "I like your receiving room. Nice access with the double doors."

"Keeps the cold and snow out of the pub," Ryan admitted. "Come on. I'll show you the rest of the place quickly, then we can eat and relax until the deliveries show up."

Madison had a blast wandering at Ryan's side and listening to him as he described what had been where, before his upgrades. The place wasn't fancy, but it had a nice calming decor, with sturdy enough stools and flooring to make maintenance a breeze.

He gestured toward the sixteen-foot-long bar counter, and she laughed softly as she settled on one of the comfortably padded, old-fashioned barstools that were firmly screwed to the floor. "You've done a fine job making the place redneck-proof."

His lips twitched up into a smile. "Well, most of the crowd who shows up isn't *too* rough around the edges. But we don't have very much that's not fastened down. No use asking for trouble."

The place was full of warm wood and black wrought iron touches, including wall sconces and strategically placed horseshoes. The sturdy chandelier hung close to the ceiling over the stage area would've looked awesome in any ranch house, and added a touch of hominess to the area.

Everywhere Madison looked she saw things that made her nod in approval. Like the restrooms labelled *Cowgirl, Cowboy, and Cowfolk.*

She met Ryan's gaze. "I like it very much. You've done a great job."

His cheeks didn't flush, but he looked pleased. "Not much else you could say, considering you're staying with me for a month."

"Oh, hotshot, you know me better than that," Madison chided. "If I see something I think you should fix, I'll be apologizing for how fast I let you know."

Ryan shrugged. "Yeah, I suppose you're right."

He pointed her to one of the low tables at the side of the room where he'd placed their Subway lunch bag. He pulled out a chair for her, then Madison portioned out their sandwiches.

"Now, before we get interrupted, you *are* going to tell me what you've been up to." Ryan said it with a great deal of firmness. "The update for the past three years since our last flurry of emails."

Madison paused before taking a bite of her sandwich. "All three years?"

"Eventually, yes," he insisted. "But for now, what have you been doing for work lately? And what's ahead of you in Toronto?"

Oh, boy. Madison considered the best place to start. "You

know I've been working in the industry pretty much since I went home to help Mom. A couple of years ago, once the boys were old enough to be a little more responsible, I started working a steady late shift at Nighthawk."

Ryan gave a low whistle at the mention of one of the most exclusive nightclubs in the Vancouver area. "High-class place. Good for you. Are you changing over to one of their sister companies in Toronto?"

Madison took a sip of her pop then nodded. "I ended up serving the night some bigwigs were in the house, and one thing led to another, and now I'm moving."

He was eyeing her now, forgotten sandwich held in midair. "How come it feels like there're a whole lot of details vital to the story that I'm not hearing?"

"Because I'm under an NDA," Madison said softly.

His expression made her lips twitch.

Utter confusion and shock. "You have a job that you had to sign a nondisclosure agreement for?"

She nodded. "I can tell you this. I'm happy with how everything turned out, and the job in Toronto will be rewarding. Plus, the timing was right for me to leave Vancouver. My family wasn't ready for me to go until now."

Ryan still looked shocked, but he was once again eating. Swallowing before he spoke, he looked resigned. "If there is anything I can do to help, I want to know."

"If there's anything I need, I will ask," Madison promised.

"I guess I'll have to take that at face value." He gestured to the pile of papers she'd placed on the tabletop. "Did you bring homework?"

"For you, yes." She pushed the information across the table. "This task was easy. Once you make a choice, I will deal with the rest of the details over the next few days. The first page shows you what the bed stats are in terms of mattress firmness and memory foam options."

He grabbed the three bundles and spread them out in front of him. "You are something else, Mad. You are seriously going to make me buy a bed."

"Unless you tell me no," she said happily. "By the way, I apologize for telling you after the fact, but I did bounce on your bed."

A snort escaped him. Ryan brushed a napkin over his mouth. "Really? When?"

"Yesterday, when you went to get groceries. I wanted to see how firm it was. If you're comfortable with what you've got now, I think those three choices will all work well."

Ryan shook his head, but he was smiling as he flipped to the second page. "Prices."

"I didn't bother to do up the quilt and sheets cost on all of them because that part will be the same no matter what. All you need to decide is which style mattress you like and whether you want a queen- or king-size."

He stacked the papers together and put them aside. Then he met her gaze. "Thank you."

"You're welcome."

The first shipment arrived shortly after that, and Madison spent a couple of lovely hours helping Ryan put away stock and update his inventory system.

During a pit stop in the little cowgirl's room, Madison noted with approval there was a discreet notice taped to the back of the stall door. *If your date is getting out of line, or if you feel unsafe and need help, go to the bar and order a White Angel. Someone will ensure that you have a safe place to go or a way to get home.*

Ryan had created a place for everyone to relax and enjoy themselves. Except assholes. Madison approved.

Fifteen minutes before they were scheduled to leave to pick up Talia, Ryan's assistant manager showed up. Grace was a tall, sturdy blonde, late thirties or early forties, with a quick smile and a firm handshake.

"So, *you're* Madison. I'm not sure if I should be looking for a halo or a set of horns, according to the stories I've heard about you," Grace teased.

"Left shoulder, right shoulder. I swear there's an angel on both." Madison winked. "How do you like the pub business?"

"It's a bit of a kick," Grace said easily. She examined Madison more intently. "Have we met before?"

"Doubtful. I've been out in Vancouver for a lot of years."

"Must be how much this one talks about you." Grace jerked a thumb toward Ryan then met his eye roll with a grin. "Not much new to catch you up on. You'll be here tomorrow night as usual?"

"Maddy and I both, yes," Ryan said. "And Saturday afternoon for the Christmas hamper stuffing."

"I've got my truck and a couple other volunteers lined up, so hamper delivery is taken care of." Grace moved efficiently behind the bar, prepping things for the evening and getting cash floats together. She waved them off. "I'll see you tomorrow, then."

They headed to leave. Ryan stepped ahead to pull the door open, and they moved together into the sunshine. The sky was still bright blue outside, but the wind had picked up.

Ryan wrapped an arm around Madison's waist, using his body as a block against the chill. "Winter has officially arrived."

A quick rush of heat slid through her, unexpected. It prickled her senses and tingled from the inside out. The scent of Ryan, the feel of his arms—

Inappropriate. The bubbling sensation of attraction wasn't welcome. Not when it was proximity to *Ryan* triggering the emotion. She was only in Heart Falls for a short time, and he was the only best friend she had.

No way was she messing that up.

Madison settled in the truck seat, took a deep breath, and told her errant body to behave.

TALIA MOVED in quasi-slow motion as she washed the dishes, head swiveling constantly to where Madison was curled up on the couch reading a book. Ryan was torn between finding his daughter's deliberate dawdling amusing or being exasperated. They couldn't get to the next part of the evening until Talia was done with her chores.

When he insisted that Madison let Talia do the job on her own, he'd gotten no complaints. At least none from Madison. "Trust me. I know how important it is for chores to get done."

She tousled Talia's hair and wished her good luck.

Ryan pulled Madison aside to introduce her to babysitter Laura. The older woman nodded a welcome before assuring Ryan she was fine with last minute adjustments to their schedule. "I'm not going anywhere this holiday season, but if you don't need me, that's okay. Just let me know."

They had returned to the kitchen to find Talia barely moving. Madison planted herself on the couch and brought out her e-reader.

Ryan went through the sample bed packages Madison had created for him one last time. The price differences weren't too extreme, and Madison had helpfully noted that he would have at least ninety days to try his purchase out to make sure that he was comfortable.

So, decision made.

And while Madison had made the task seem easy, he knew if *he'd* had to get to this point, with the Google search and dredging through information, it would've been a minimum of two weeks before he'd have been ready to order.

If he'd actually started in the first place.

He put the information about the bed he wanted on the coffee table then slipped the other two packages onto the bookshelf. He'd recycle them once the one he'd selected was approved.

"Madison," Talia said quietly.

Maddy glanced up from the couch. "You done?"

Talia glanced at the big pot still sitting on the counter and sighed dramatically. Then she turned back, a little more eagerness in her tone. "Almost. You said you had pictures. Can we look at them tonight?"

"Sure." Madison glanced at Ryan. "Unless there's something else that needs to be done?"

"Anything else on your chore chart?" Ryan asked Talia.

She glanced at the fridge where the grid for both their house tasks were clearly labelled. "I have to sort my laundry into the right piles, but that will only take a minute."

Madison sat forward. "Okay. I'll go get the pictures and bring them back here to the couch. Once you're done, you can join me. Sound good?"

Talia all but shouted *yes* as she bobbed up and down on the step stool, scrubbing the final pot vigorously.

Madison paused as she passed Ryan at the entrance to the hallway, leaning in close to whisper in his ear, "I remember my brothers at this age. They constantly tried to get out of chores. They always had something vital that they needed to do. Or some story that they *had* to tell me that was life or death."

"Sometimes it feels as if doing the task myself would be so much simpler, but I know in the long run, it's better if she learns," Ryan agreed quietly.

She chuckled, the soft sound brushing against him as her warm breath skimmed his cheek. "Kids are amazing. And terrible, *and* wonderful."

Ryan barely registered what she'd said. Something inside him tumbled, his gut tightening. He was already moving, ready to catch hold of her hips and pull her tight against him when she stepped away and disappeared down the hall.

What the hell?

He turned on the spot and paced across the room to the front door. A moment later he stood on the porch in his shirtsleeves, the frigid December wind barely enough to cool him off.

He took a deep breath and let the sharp bite of the cold knock the cobwebs from his brain.

Lust. Putting a name to the sensation didn't make it better. Recognizing the sensation wasn't good either, although it had been a long time since he'd felt it so sharp and clear.

The door opened behind him. Talia stared up at him with her big, brown eyes, perplexed. "You don't have a coat on."

He forced a chuckle, turned, and firmly closed and locked the door behind himself. "Thought I heard something. Nothing there. Maybe it was Santa doing a practice run."

Very impressively, Talia raised one single brow. "*Daddy*."

"What?"

With the teeniest hint of attitude, she tilted her head and gave him a look. "You don't have to pretend about Santa anymore."

"Hey, I don't make the rules. As long as *somebody* still thinks the old elf flies around delivering presents at Christmas, magic reindeer and all the rest, I'm going to talk as if it's true."

Talia rolled her eyes. "He's. Not. Real."

Before he could respond again, she'd raced over to Madison and dropped onto the couch beside her.

Madison glanced at him over the top of her glass as she took a drink.

Talia had said it pointedly, not rudely, so he let it go, offering his friend a gentle shrug of his shoulders. Not rude, but one more step on the changing path of his little girl to something other than fantasy stories and magic.

The thought made him a little sad this time. He wasn't sure *he* was ready to let that go.

Madison opened the photo album in her lap, turning to Talia. "Here we go. I told you I knew you when you were baby. Look."

She pointed to the page.

Talia popped up on her knees and leaned against Madison's side, nose hovering over the page of the book. "Is that me?"

"Yep. And this is your mommy, and here is Daddy."

A little-girl laugh rang out. Thankfully, the haughtiness of a few moments earlier had vanished. Talia glanced up at Ryan, who had sat down opposite them. "Daddy. You don't look like this anymore."

"I bet you don't look like you did ten years ago, either," Ryan teased.

"Come see," Talia ordered.

He crossed over to the couch, but when he would've sat beside Talia, she pushed him toward the open space on the other side of Madison. "Madison in the middle. Then we can both see."

It was the most natural thing in the world, sitting next to Madison. Looking through old photographs from when he'd been so full of happiness and his world held nothing but potential. His beloved wife and new baby. A good friend returned for a short but sweet visit, because it was as long as she could get away for.

Ryan fell into thought for a moment as Madison flipped through pages and showed Talia more pictures. Some from their days at college, some with her family.

Talia was awed by a picture with Madison, her two brothers, and her parents. "They're so little. Your brothers are like babies compared to you."

"That's because they *were* babies," Madison told her. "I was twelve years old when Joe and Kyle were born."

The little girl blinked. "Wow." She concentrated for a minute. "That's even older than me."

"Yep."

"Did they cry a lot?"

Madison leaned back on the couch and took a deep breath. "Oh, boy, did they ever. But they grew out of it, and now they're nearly grown up, and they're wonderful people."

"Who's this?" Talia pointed at Madison's parents.

"That is my mom and dad," Madison told her simply.

"Do they still live in Vancouver?"

"My mom does. She lives with my brothers. My dad died a long time ago."

Talia froze. She looked up at Madison's face and then back at the pictures. "Just like my mommy. That happened a long time ago, too."

"It did. In fact, my dad died about a year before your mom did, so it was a sad time for us all."

Talia cuddled up against Madison's side, curling her arms around her arm and squeezing tight. "I still get sad that Mommy's not here."

"Makes sense. I still miss my daddy, and I miss your mom, but I have lots of good memories. That's what I try to think about when I get sad."

"I don't really have memories of Mommy," Talia whispered. "I was only a baby."

"I know, sweetie," Madison said, squeezing an arm around her. "But that's the good part of memories. We can share them. I'll share some nice memories of your mommy with you while I'm here, okay?"

The entire time this conversation was going on, Ryan listened quietly. It was so simple and sweet and heartbreaking at the same time. He had zero worries that Madison was going to say something wrong—

What he was more perturbed about were the sensations rising up and interrupting his thoughts over and over.

This wasn't the time to be so utterly aware of his thigh

pressed against Madison's. Or of how, as she turned the photo album pages, her elbow brushed his biceps, the heat of their torsos connecting.

Talia had reached over Madison and was tugging on his sleeve. Guilt washed over him. "I'm sorry, little one. What did you say?"

"Did Mommy like Christmastime?"

Ryan nodded. "Very much. Not just Christmas Day, but the whole holiday season. She liked decorating, and she really liked dressing up and having a fancy dinner on New Year's."

Answering the question let him focus on something other than the too-vivid physical reaction of his body. What the hell was going on that even the gentle scent wafting off Madison—something clean with a hint of orange—was making him lose all focus?

When the evening came to an end, and his little girl was tucked into bed, Ryan made sure to keep a safe distance between him and Madison as they quietly sat and worked on different things.

She caught up with her brothers, he answered some emails.

Quiet, cozy...intimate.

When Madison finally said good night and left the room, Ryan wasn't sure if it was relief or dread he felt.

7

Friday was one of the busiest days on Ryan's schedule, and Madison had no intention of trying to keep up with him.

At breakfast she laid out her plans. "Since you're at the fire hall the entire time Talia's at school, I thought I might check out some of those highlights Brooke mentioned. If I could get a ride downtown."

"Not a problem," Ryan assured her. "Buns and Roses is a great place for lunch."

"I might end up there. Brooke called to tell me the replacement airbag for my car is in. She plans to install it this morning." Talia popped up on her chair, hands pressed to the table. Madison handed Talia the plate of toast the little girl was reaching for. "While she's working, I'll look around."

"Sounds like a plan. We'll be heading straight to my parents' after I pick Talia up from school. You're welcome to come, of course," Ryan offered.

It was easy to smile. "I wouldn't miss it for anything," Madison assured him, glancing at Talia. She'd save the conversation about the ballet idea for when she and Ryan had some privacy.

Madison quickly put in the order for the mattress Ryan had selected as morning activity whirled around her.

They dropped Talia off at school then Ryan took Madison to the Heart Falls auto shop. "Call me if you need anything," Ryan told her sternly.

"Yes, sir," she offered with a wink before stepping across the snowy packing lot and into the warm waiting area.

Brooke waved a welcome from where she'd stood beside Madison's open car door. She wiped her hands on a rag as she made her way to the front counter.

The brunette's welcome was warm and sincere. "I'm going to replace the airbag, but my dad's going to do the rest of the checkup. I wondered if you wanted to hit the coffee shop with me while he's working?"

"I need a job like yours," Madison teased. "But if you can get away, that would be great."

Brooke gestured at the open spaces in the shop. "When it's full, we work. This is the calm before the storm, probably literally, considering it's December. My dad said he wanted time off next week, which means I get time off today."

"Great system." Madison gazed around the shiny shop with all the high-tech machinery lined up beside old-fashioned benches and what looked like archaic instruments of torture.

While Brooke worked, Madison bundled herself up and went for a walk down Main Street, trying to get a feel for the place.

It was cold but clear, the sky overhead a robin's-egg blue. Every breath she took was sharp against the back of her throat, and clouds formed on every exhale. She pulled gloves out of her pocket, adjusted her hat a little more firmly in place and walked briskly.

Main Street was lined with cars parked on the angle and a

wide sidewalk on one side. The opposite side had been built with a fancy boardwalk and access ramps strategically located along the length. Window displays ran the gamut from tiny villages with sparkling lights and pretend snow to the oddly located Mercantile where somebody had created the underside of a lake. A giant fishing hook had been lowered through a layer of pretend ice, and a selection of fish wearing Santa hats hung suspended at different levels, eyeing it suspiciously.

Rough Cut was along the boardwalk side, windows traced with fake snow in the corners. Broad wooden shutters framed the glass on each side, and a calendar/menu board had a background of fake black diamonds.

Madison leaned in closer to check the schedule. She noted with approval that Ryan had nightly food specials, but he also had a couple of regular afternoon activities posted. Cribbage on Tuesdays, and the quilters' guild on Wednesday.

"Madison. *Madison*."

She spun in shock at hearing Talia's high-pitched, little-girl voice.

Relief set in as she noticed her waving frantically as she walked in a lineup with her friends, all headed into one of the stores down the street. Madison waved back then followed.

They had slipped into a bookstore, and Madison realized it was the one Brooke had mentioned in her list of things to do. The overhead bell chimed softly as Madison entered and stopped.

The class was all gathered to one side of the room, settling onto a wide carpeted area as a stately gentleman with dark skin and neatly trimmed, silvering-at-the-temples black hair settled into a chair in front of them. "Welcome to Fallen Books, grade four students. Just a reminder: I'm Malachi Fields."

"Hello, Mr. Fields," the entire class chorused somewhat in unison.

"I'm glad you came back. Today we're going to talk about

traditions from different parts of the world." He pulled some brightly coloured books off the display from beside him and began showing off pictures and telling stories about how different cultures celebrated milestones.

Madison watched for a moment, smiling as she saw Talia shooting up her hand to answer questions and talking quietly with the little girl next to her.

The store was full of beautiful, tempting books, including a thriller she'd been considering. Madison planned to come back to check it out very soon.

But now she slipped quietly away before she disturbed the class. Returning to her exploration of Heart Falls, she checked her watch to make sure she was back at the mechanic's shop in time to join Brooke.

Her new friend was behind the counter. She put down the paperwork she was filling out, grabbed a coat off the wall and got dressed quickly. "Let's go before you get overheated and have to take off all your stuff."

Madison held the door for her. "It is nippy out here. I'd forgotten how cold Alberta is in the winter."

"Vancouver area still gets cold, doesn't it?" Brooke asked.

"Cold and damp, which is a special kind of nasty, but not *this* cold very often," Madison told her. "And I don't know if you get colder weather here than Edmonton, because that's where I mostly lived."

They paced side by side down Main Street to where the cozy coffee shop called Buns and Roses sat. Warm, golden light shone out the windows, and the most amazing scent filled Madison's soul as they stepped inside.

"Yum. I think I'm just going to stand here and breathe deep for about half an hour," Madison said.

Brooke laughed, catching Madison by the arm and tugging her toward a small table—one of the only available in the entire space. "That would be zero calories, but trust me, you want to indulge in the real thing."

Behind the counter, two women were rapidly filling orders. The one with blonde hair and cream-white skin wore pigtails high on her head and had attached bells to hold them in place. Every time she moved, the bells rang, which meant she jingled almost constantly. She had a wide smile and chatted easily with the people she served.

The second woman was a contrast. She still looked approachable, but more in a regal matter instead of a ready-to-be-your-best-buddy kind of way. She had the most fantastic skin Madison had ever seen. Deep brown with a shimmering glow that made her look as if she were ready to head down a fashion runway. Long, dark-brown hair hung in a braid over her shoulder, and she wore a Santa hat as she worked the espresso machine.

"Tansy is on the left," Brooke told her. "Her sister, Rose, is making the coffees."

Madison hesitated for a moment. The two women were seemingly not related by blood. "Talia mentioned Rose was one of the people Ryan works with."

"The food bank," Brooke explained. "Co-coordinators. We'll see her tomorrow afternoon when we're putting together the hampers."

It took some concentration for Madison to drag her gaze to the handwritten menu on the wall instead of staring at the very beautiful Rose. Obviously, she was someone to place on the list of potential women for Ryan to date, considering he worked with her.

An uneasy sensation tickled Madison's insides.

By the time they'd received their order, though, Madison had gotten herself straightened out again. Part of it was because Brooke was so easy to spend time with.

Brooke had just finished describing her and Mack's wedding and the ensuing honeymoon trip they had taken to Universal Studios. The other woman leaned back in her chair, both hands cupped around her coffee. "Wow. Ryan warned me about this, but I thought he was joking."

"About what?" Madison was tempted to pick up her plate and lick the cinnamon sugar crumbs off it. Instead, she pressed her fingertip into the biggest clumps and transferred them to her mouth that way. It was probably rude, but they were really too good to waste.

Brooke lifted a finger and shook it slowly. "You ask a question, then I spent the next ten minutes answering it. Then I ask you a question and somehow, in the space of about two sentences, you've got me talking again."

And Ryan had warned her about this? Too funny. Madison met Brooke's gaze straight on and asked with an absolutely straight face, "And why do you think that is?"

The laugh that burst from Brooke drew attention from people sitting around them. She sat forward as well, putting her coffee cup on the table. "I like you."

A warm glow buzzed in Madison's belly. "I like you, too."

Her phone buzzed on the table. Normally, she would've ignored it, but a quick glance said that it was her brother, and this was not when he should be calling.

She glanced up at Brooke and apologized. "Sorry, I have to take this."

"No problem. I'll grab us dessert."

Madison rose from the table and headed toward the hallway where the bathrooms were to have a little privacy and not disrupt the rest of the café. "Joe?"

There was just the faintest quiver of panic in his voice, along with a ton of frustration. "Hey, Mad. Sorry for calling, but can you talk to this registrant for me? They say there's a problem with my classes for next semester, and I can't figure out how to fix it."

Damn. "Sure, kiddo. It's probably just a computer glitch. Don't worry," she assured him.

"Okay. Here she is." He already sounded better. As if he knew Madison wouldn't let him down.

Fortunately, it was a computer issue, easily solved once the registrant realized she was trying to update the class list for a *Josephine Joy,* whose student number was only two transposed digits different than Joe's.

Joe came back on the line, his tone low. "Thank you. She doesn't look very happy right now."

"Mistakes happen. And now we know you're confirmed for some fantastic classes that will provide enough homework to keep you out of trouble." Madison made her way back toward the table where Brooke was placing plates in front of both their chairs. "You okay now?"

"Yeah. Love you," Joe said quickly. "Talk later."

Madison sat down and put her phone aside, eyeing the enormous brownie covered with what looked to be almost an inch of icing. "Will you marry me?"

Brooke snickered softly before meeting Madison's eyes. "Everything okay?"

Slicing off a small portion and stabbing it with her fork, Madison examined the rich gooiness as the scent of chocolate teased her. "Everything's fine. One of my brothers was having problems with his university schedule. We got it straightened out."

"Glad it was something simple." Brooke took a bite of her own brownie and made a happy noise. "*One* of your brothers. You have more?"

"Two. A matched set. They turned eighteen last June and are now exploring the wonderful world of higher education."

Madison took the first mouthful and groaned. When she could talk again, she simply pointed her fork at the brownie. "Wow."

"I know, right? Just wait. If you're going to be around this month, I'll bring you to girls' night out. Tansy always bakes something so good; it will knock your socks off." Brooke switched back to her coffee. "So, now that you know everything about me, my husband, how long I've lived in Heart Falls, what kind of appliances I have in my house—that was a really weird conversation twist, by the way—I want to know more about you."

"Friend of Ryan's since forever," Madison said. "Two brothers, one mom. Dad passed away a number of years ago. I've been a bartender for most of my adult life, and I am really looking forward to having a relaxing time here in Heart Falls over the holidays."

Brooke was nodding slowly. "And in under a minute, you just told me more than you told me in the forty-five minutes before."

Madison shrugged. "I'm curious about people. I already know things about myself. I don't need to talk about *me*."

The other woman laughed along with her. "Yeah, well, usually people *like* to talk about themselves. I think you're very interesting, Madison Joy. I want to get together again to find out more."

"Then it's a good thing I'll be staying in Heart Falls over the holidays, isn't it?" Madison said as a warm glow of happiness rushed in.

That glow lingered through the rest of the meal and going to pick up her car from the shop.

Spending time with Ryan was why she had come to Heart Falls, but when she thought about it more during the afternoon as she made some notes for Ryan's possible fundraiser, Madison had to admit she'd been thinking too small.

Getting to spend time with someone like Brooke was

important as well. Time with good girlfriends was something Madison had missed just as much over the past years.

She was going to say yes to every opportunity she was offered. Soak in friendship and family, such as it was.

Madison Joy was going to grab on with both hands and live life to the fullest.

8

Having picked up Talia from school, Ryan concentrated on getting them safely onto the highway and let his daughter chatter at Madison.

"And I have to practice again at Nâinai and Yéyé's. I can show you where I need help so I don't bump into the wall." Talia tapped on the back of Madison's seat. "Do you want to stay at my grandparents' tonight?"

Before Ryan could suggest that might not be a good idea, Madison beat him to it.

"I like your grandparents," Madison said, glancing over her shoulder. "But if I were going to stay, I should have asked them earlier. And I would've had to make sure I brought the things I needed with me for a visit."

"But you didn't tell Daddy before you came for a visit," Talia pointed out.

Madison glanced at him, and they made a brief eye contact. "You're right, Talia, and it was rude. I'm not going to be rude to your grandparents."

"But they won't mind," Talia insisted.

"Talia. That's enough," Ryan said firmly. "You're both right.

Madison should've told me ahead of time that she was coming, and we're going to learn a lesson from that. We'll see if a longer visit with Nâinai and Yéyé works at some point."

His daughter sat back, slightly disgruntled.

Definitely a good moment for a distraction. "Something else we need to talk about is your birthday. We need to decide what day to celebrate so we can ask your friends to your party."

Madison twisted in her chair seat. "That's right. Your birthday is coming up very soon."

Silence from the back seat.

Very unexpected response. Ryan glanced back momentarily to discover Talia staring out the window. "Little one? Did you hear me?"

An enormous sigh left Talia. It was so big, Ryan imagined if he glanced over his shoulder, he'd find nothing but a deflated balloon strapped into her booster seat. Then she spoke, quiet but clear. "I don't want a party."

Madison frowned but didn't say anything.

Maybe this wasn't the best topic to discuss while they were driving on the highway. Usually, though, Ryan found he could bring up any topic, and Talia would talk nearly the entire hour-and-a-half-long trip.

Birthday party plans should have still been spilling out of Talia when they were pulling into his parents' driveway.

Ryan looked for a solution but decided this would be a good moment to put off until he could give it his full attention. "Well, you give it some more thought, and after the weekend, we'll figure out what you want to do."

In the rearview mirror, Talia's lips pinched together into a straight line as if she were forcing herself to stay silent.

Fortunately that lasted for all of fifteen seconds, although when she started talking, it wasn't about any birthday plans. "Madison, I saw you today. When I was on my field trip."

"I saw you, too," Madison replied, and thankfully

conversation returned to a chattering Talia, a laughing Madison, and him…

One slightly confused male who really hoped, at some point, someone would explain to him what was going on.

His parents' home was a small duplex three blocks from the hospital. They were all greeted with hugs, including Madison, who was enveloped by Ryan's mother as if she were a long-lost child.

"Sweet Madison. I was so glad when Ryan said you would come visit." His mother's head only came up to Madison's chin, but they hugged each other tightly, his father standing to the side, waiting his turn.

Madison had closed her eyes, a soft smile on her face. She looked as if she were soaking in the hugs, first from his mom, then his dad.

She stepped away from them, shaking her head slightly. "I've missed you both very much. But I've sent up many good wishes and good thoughts over the years. I'm glad to see you looking so wonderful."

"And you." His mom held on to Madison's hand as she eyed Madison closer. Mom clicked her tongue. "Except you're too skinny. Come. Tonight I'll feed you a *proper* meal."

"Madison has to see my room," Talia insisted.

Ryan's father raised a brow. "Madison can come with you as you take your bag to your room. Then you can both wash your hands and join us at the table."

Madison exchanged glances with Ryan. She was smiling from ear to ear. "It's just like we're back in high school."

"I hope not. I don't want to have to come to the principal's office *again* to hear how you two have been distracting classes," his mother said sternly. She turned to Ryan and pointed at the kitchen. "Go. Wash your hands, then you can help put the food on the table."

Laughter escaped Madison as she scooped up Talia's bag,

fingers linked with Talia as the little girl tugged Maddy off to her bedroom.

It was like going back in time. Other than the fact that they were all older, and Talia was there, that wonderful feeling of comfort had returned.

Throughout the meal, Madison did it again. That thing of finding out exactly from everyone else what they'd been up to while not saying a word about her own plans. Her own past.

They were at the front door preparing to head back to Heart Falls when his mother caught Madison in another hug. "You will come to visit again while you're here," she ordered.

"Yes, Mother," Madison said brightly.

Talia was still on the quiet side, but she came and hugged Ryan fiercely, pressing a huge smack of a kiss to his cheek. When he put her down, she headed to Madison, arms out wide.

Madison knelt. "Yes? Is this another one of your dance positions?"

Talia didn't move. just kept her arms stretched to the sides. "You're supposed to hug me," his daughter informed her.

"Oh. I suppose I can do that," Madison said. Only first, she scrunched the hair on the top of Talia's head, and then in the middle of the hug, one of them started to tickle the other, because giggling broke out.

It was a far happier leaving than expected.

Madison waited until they were back on the main road before she started talking. "Your parents are wonderful. Your mom's cooking is fantastic, and they seem to be really happy in their home. And your Dad looks like he's doing okay."

"He is. He just needs to monitor things." Ryan started mentally going through the rest of the evening, which wouldn't officially start until they showed up at Rough Cut.

"You okay to do some brainstorming while we drive?" Madison asked.

"Sure. About what?"

Of course, she started with the bomb. "What was that about? Talia not wanting a birthday party? Her birthday is on Christmas Day. When do you usually celebrate?"

"She gets a birthday cake on the twenty-fifth, but we usually have a party the week before, depending on when school is out for the holiday break." Ryan shrugged. "I really have no idea what's going on. Last week she was making noises about wanting a sleepover, so this idea of no party? We'll figure that out when she's home on Sunday."

"Just remember I'm available to help with whatever," Madison said. She changed topics completely. "I have an idea for your fundraiser."

Ryan blinked. "Okay."

"It also means that Talia and her friends will get to do their dance recital." Madison twisted to face him, adjusting the seat belt so that it would still work. "I talked to Charity, and that part is just fine."

Ryan shook his head slightly. "You still have only one speed, don't you? Full-out engaged."

"Yep," Madison agreed. "Do you know *The Nutcracker*?"

For a second, he was lost until he realized she was talking about the ballet. He made a face. "Not personally."

"Perfect. Now, you know how at some country fairs, you pay money to try and drop people into the dunk tank?"

What was she up to? "Yes, but it's currently December in Alberta. I don't think hypothermia is a good thing to play with."

"It's the *other* part I'm thinking about. The bit where people are willing to pay money to watch somebody do something uncomfortable. In this case, I'm not talking about getting dumped into water but having to go up on a stage."

"Go on." Because even if it came to nothing, watching Madison's brain at work was a beautiful thing.

She leaned against the dashboard and grinned before sitting back. "Okay, so I can't take full credit for this, because one of my brothers was involved in a wacky *Nutcracker* performance years ago, and I thought it was pretty smart."

"I don't know the story of the Nutcracker," Ryan warned her.

"That's good. Because this is going to be nothing like the usual version," she said with a laugh. "The idea is we have an outline of a story, and different people perform each scene. Which means zero group practices and a very simple performance day. I'll explain the logistics later, but what we need to do is come up with a variation on *The Nutcracker* that's going to work for your community."

"I thought *The Nutcracker* was very traditional."

Madison shrugged. "For some people, sure. For us, we should do what's going to work best. Which means we come up with some great scenes that you would absolutely put down money to get one of your friends to star in. For example, how much would you pay to see Brad Ford pretend to be a daisy blowing in the breeze?"

A snort escaped before Ryan could stop it. "Dear God. Where do I sign up to put my twenty bucks?"

Madison rubbed her hands together. "See? Now you're getting the swing of it. Let me worry about the details, but let's brainstorm for a minute."

"For your nontraditional Nutcracker story?"

"Definitely. Here's a very, very basic outline that I want to mess up—and there are a million variations on this plot already. This is just the one I think will work the best for us."

He didn't say anything while she went through a list that included magical dolls, a Nutcracker, and toy soldiers, but when she mentioned a Mouse King, he finally had something to suggest. "If you want this to be properly local, it's not a mouse as the villain, it's a rat."

Her smile bloomed. "You're right. There are no rats in Alberta."

"And if anyone is going to *fight* a Rat King, it should be the rat patrol."

Madison pulled a notebook out of somewhere and was eagerly taking down notes. "Keep going. After they defeat the Rat King, the soldier turns into a handsome prince and takes them to the land of sweets. That's where the girls will be dancing."

"The rat patrol wouldn't go to the land of sweets," Ryan said with a laugh. "They'd probably go to a magical barn."

She whooped and wrote it down. "Perfect. Which means instead of having dancing candies, we're going to have dancing barn animals."

"Dear God, my friends are going to kill us. This is amazing," Ryan said happily.

"You don't have to sound so delighted," Madison said, but she was laughing as well.

"Trust me, this is a good thing," Ryan assured her.

"Tell me." Her tone was a lot more serious for a moment. "Do you think your friends would be willing? Not just to put up money, but to actually perform if somebody ponies up the money under *their* name?"

Ryan thought about it for a moment and nodded briskly. "I think most of them will push to the front of the line to volunteer."

She looked delighted. "Then I will get things together, and we can start with a volunteer sign-up list tomorrow during the Christmas hamper event."

He reached across and grabbed her hand, squeezing tight. "You come up with this stuff all the time and make it look so easy. But I'm really glad you've put your creative energy toward something that's going to make a difference in my hometown. Thank you."

She looked surprised for a moment. "Of course. You're welcome."

The last part of the trip passed quickly as Madison continued to toss out ideas, Ryan responding. By the time they pulled into the parking lot outside Rough Cut, Madison was putting the finishing touches on her first draft for the performance.

In the parking lot before they headed inside, Ryan was astonished when Madison cut him off. She wrapped her arms around him, smiling up at him with delight written all over her face. "I had so much fun. Thank you."

She hugged him, a huge squeeze of her arms around his torso, her face pressed against his chest.

Ryan held on and soaked it in. "I had fun, too."

He had, and it was the truth, but there was another truth rising. As his nose brushed strands of her hair, the scent of her shampoo and unique fragrance from her skin stirred something inside. There were layers between them—so many layers, because it was a cold December day, which meant clothes and coats and scarves.

He shouldn't be so utterly aware of her as a woman.

In his arms. Soft yet strong.

She gave a final squeeze before easing back and kissing him. A firm press of her lips against his cheek before she released him completely and headed to the door.

Oblivious to the fact she'd just detonated a bomb somewhere in his core.

Somehow Ryan made his feet move. Stumbled after her without falling over, because his body didn't seem to be functioning properly. His cheek tingled, and his legs were unsteady—

Other parts of his anatomy had reacted as well, and that just wasn't right. The cold day, all the clothing, all the rest of it. It was like two snowmen making contact, and yet...

Ryan took a deep breath, and the cutting edge of winter chill raced down his throat and into his lungs, harsh enough to make him cough. Make him tense up from physical pain instead of the sensual arousal of his body.

No. They'd just spent an hour and a half talking about dancing cows, for fuck's sake. He was not going to let this inexplicably erratic lust that kept striking out of the blue ruin their relationship.

Ryan followed Madison into the bar, making himself as cold inside as possible. Best friends. They were best friends. *Period*.

His body ached, and his brain offered up a hundred different excuses why getting involved was actually a good idea.

Good thing he had a job to do.

9

Things turned around pretty quickly once Ryan threw himself wholeheartedly into pub work as a distraction. It helped that Madison got hauled off by Grace to assist behind the bar as the evening turned into one of their busiest in recent history.

After staying up until two a.m., both he and Madison slept in late on Saturday morning.

Ryan managed to wake up before her, which was a good thing on many fronts. First, it let him go for a run and get some stretching in, which always helped him find a peaceful center. The attraction he felt made all kinds of sense. Madison was a beautiful woman, and now that he'd started to think about dating, it was only logical that his long-denied sexual urges would start to rise to the surface.

Knowing the sparks when he looked at her were natural meant he could give the urges a nod yet keep his damn hands to himself.

The more important thing he needed to do before Madison woke up was find a way to stash the ugly holiday sweater where she would find it. Because it had been a few days since she'd ensnared him, she should no longer be as cautious. He could hardly wait for it to be her turn to have to wear it out in public.

He was back on the floor of the living room, leaning over his outstretched leg when she shuffled into the room. Neon-green socks on her feet this time, Madison yawned and stretched. Her sweatshirt rode up, revealing a line of bare stomach, and a hard thump registered somewhere near his groin.

Ignoring the hormones racing through him, Ryan grinned. "You were a lot more tired than I expected."

She checked the coffee machine. "I haven't been on a late-night routine for a while. Is this ready to turn on?"

"Yep. Just hit start." He pondered her comment for a moment. "How have you been working at the bar without staying up late?"

Madison twisted and leaned back on the counter as the coffee machine began making bubbling noises beside her. She yawned again, arching her back, and her sweatshirt stretched across her breasts. "I haven't actually worked at the bar since September."

Okay.

Ryan got to his feet and approached Madison, ignoring the urge to examine every inch of her. If he'd finally managed to get her to start talking, he was going to roll with it. "Maddy. Without breaking your NDA, can you tell me a little more? Are you okay? How on earth could you not have worked since September and still be financially fine?"

The scent of coffee drifted on the air. A fan buzzed somewhere in the back rooms of his house, but it was the slow intake of breath and the even slower exhale that he heard in minute detail. It was her nibbling on her bottom lip as she fought to figure out what to share.

Screw this. Ryan tugged her into his arms and held her close. Her body was tight for a moment, shoulders rigid, spine straight. He rubbed a hand up and down her back and made shushing noises until she relaxed just the slightest bit, leaning against him harder and taking a deep breath. He spoke quietly, as reassuringly as he could. "I'm not trying to make things more stressful. Just tell me this. Whatever the hell is going on, is it a good thing?"

She buried her face against his neck, humming as if happy. "It's good. Really, don't worry about me. That damn NDA."

They just stood there, holding each other, until the coffee gurgled its final offering into the pot.

Ryan was pleased that it was all about comfort right then. Nothing sexual distracted him from being able to give a moment of support to his good friend.

Madison patted his shoulder then pushed him back a bit. "As soon as I can tell you, I will. I swear."

"I'm glad. Because I want to know," Ryan said.

Mischief in her eyes, Madison tilted her head toward the cupboard. "You get the cups. I'll get the cream."

He opened the cabinet door to discover a new set of misshapen coffee mugs. A herd of zombie snowmen, partially melted and with terrible expressions on their faces. "*Maddy.*"

"Merry Christmas," she said with a grin, tugging open the fridge without looking. A second later she let out a shriek. "Ryan Xavier Zhao."

He couldn't keep a straight face. Not when she reached in and pulled out the sweater. He'd strategically rolled it up so the Christmas decoration with the reindeer sticking out its tongue was front and center. "Merry Christmas," he repeated back to her.

They stood there with their wacky holiday items in their hands, grinning at each other, and Ryan couldn't have been happier.

Except, he corrected himself, when she walked out of her

guest room hours later, prepared to head to the Christmas hamper event, wearing the sweater.

"Payback is so sweet," he informed her.

She'd braided her hair so that pigtails fell on either side of her head, and she wore a jaunty Santa hat. The faintest hint of a bright-yellow T-shirt showed under the gaudy cardigan, and instead of her jeans, she wore stretchy yoga pants that fit her very nicely.

Very nicely.

Ryan deliberately focused on the bright-yellow socks that matched the T-shirt. "If you fall headfirst into a snowbank, we'll be able to find you."

"Only if I kick off my boots," Madison said with a laugh. "Come on. I'm ready to make my fashion debut."

Grace was already at the bar, and so was Rose. The two of them were busy assembling boxes and taping the bottoms firmly in position.

Ryan took Madison's coat and went to hang it up with his own. "Let me know what I need to get ready," he said to Rose as he passed.

"Everything's lined up, you just need to put the boxes we prepped the other day on the tables according to the labels," Rose told him.

He had just grabbed the first box when he spotted Madison. She'd paused beside the ladies and was holding out a hand to Rose.

"Hi. We haven't officially met yet, although I did see you at the coffee shop yesterday. I'm Madison."

"Nice to meet you. Rose Fields."

"Sorry," Ryan said as he hurried back. "I keep forgetting you don't know everybody," he said to Madison.

"By the end of the night, everybody will know her," Grace muttered. She used a finger to circle as she pointed at Madison. "That's the kind of outfit that gets people talking."

Madison laughed as she twirled in a circle. "It's an old tradition that I decided to re-inflict on Ryan. But as you see, what goes around, comes around."

Rose was eyeing him with the oddest expression on her face.

They'd held most of their meetings over the past years at Buns and Roses, and he'd always found her to be both quiet and efficient. He enjoyed working with her on the community hamper projects. She was a little *too* quiet in some ways, though. Too much like him in that they could drift off into their own thoughts.

"I remember somebody else wearing hideous sweaters last year," Rose said suddenly. "And I seem to remember that it was Ryan's fault."

"I've no idea what you're talking about," he offered before pointing to the corner. "Oh, look, boxes for me to tote."

The women all laughed as he moved off with a grin.

Madison fit in comfortably with any group. It was clear not only as she chipped in and helped him finish prepping the room but as people arrived, voices rising and mixing with the Christmas music he'd put on in the background. Madison greeted people, explained the routine for loading hampers. Explained the ugly sweater a dozen times with amazing good humour.

Someone had brought Christmas cookies, and someone else had apple cider, and soon the entire place smelled like Christmas.

Brooke and Mack arrived. Ryan came forward to greet his friends. "I wondered if you'd gotten an emergency callout."

Mack shook his head. "Not me. Brooke had another tow truck job at the last minute."

"Nothing serious," Brooke assured Ryan as she pushed off her heavy winter coat and turned to face him.

Ryan got a glimpse of what she was wearing and coughed.

He glanced at Mack to discover his friend had removed his outerwear and now stood next to Brooke, arm around her so it was impossible to miss how glaringly hideous their outfits were.

Mack grinned. "Nothing to say?"

"You guys are hysterical," Ryan said dryly.

Brooke gestured to the lights poking out of her sweater, obviously proud as she then pushed a button along the hemline and the LEDs started flashing merrily. "Well, last year you insisted we were supposed to dress up in our finest festive wear. You didn't announce a change of dress code, so, *voila*."

Her sweater was a Christmas tree, fully decorated, including the lights that were leaving bright spots on his retinas. Mack's sweater was slightly tamer, with small boxes tied to the surface everywhere.

"This is awesome." Madison said, stepping up behind Ryan to stare happily at Brooke and Mack. She bumped her hip against Ryan's. "You have very cool friends."

Brooke shook her head in amazement as she realized Madison was now wearing the sweater Ryan had worn at the fire hall. She looked up at Madison. "Does this mean he hid the sweater and you found it?"

"Get used to seeing this thing," Madison warned happily. "We have not yet concluded the challenge."

Mack frowned for a moment. "Does this mean we might end up seeing Ryan wearing it in the middle of summer? Because I'm not sure I'm okay with that."

Ryan shook his head. "Rules of the challenge say December only. I tried to convince her we should stop as of Christmas Day, but Madison mentioned something about Ukrainian Christmas, and it was easier to compromise and say nothing outside December."

"Good to know." Brooke gave Mack a final squeeze then stepped aside, moving toward Madison. "Let's get started so you and I can resume chatting. We have to be done before six o'clock. Is that right?"

"Pub opens then, yes," Ryan said.

Madison led her off. Ryan watched for a moment, but it was clear she didn't need him running interference. She fit in with his friends.

She fit in with him.

It was a slightly disturbing thought after how much energy he had put into making sure he had dealt with the whole lust issue, so he pushed it aside, motioning for Mack to join him. They joined the lineup of people picking up food products and loading them into individual boxes. Chatting easily.

Nothing but here and now. Because that was simpler than trying to untangle the confusion that rose every time he thought about Madison. His good friend. His best friend.

Or was she something more?

It was clear the people who'd come to Rough Cut that afternoon had done this before. The group gathered to assemble the food hampers didn't need much direction, looping through the lineup multiple times as the stack of filled food boxes beside the front door grew. Beside Madison, Brooke chatted easily, which was good because Madison was not at her best.

She was distracted and not very proud of the reason why. Jealousy had rushed in unexpectedly, and in very intense measures.

Rose Fields was one of the most beautiful women she had seen in her life.

But...so what? This hard knot inside Madison's belly shouldn't be there.

It's not as if she hadn't spent time around beautiful people.

Heck, Justina had been gorgeous as well, and yet all Madison could think of after meeting her new friend was how she hoped the other woman was as shiny on the inside as she was on the out. And when Justina proved to be an awesome person, all Madison had wanted to do was introduce her to Ryan because she just *knew* that they belonged together.

Seeing Rose chat innocently with Ryan—

Madison deliberately turned away and focused on Brooke and Yvette, who had joined them. "Good turnout to help with the hampers."

Yvette leaned past her to grab a package of spaghetti and add it to her box. "It's a busy season, so the committee suggested nothing longer than a two-hour timeframe. Makes it easier for more people to commit to come out."

That was a good point. Madison was still trying to juggle all the details for the fundraiser, but this seemed like a good time to ask. "So an event that lasts maybe an hour and a half would get people coming?"

"If there's food involved, definitely."

"Pie? Cake? Cookies? Would those be enough?" It was a doable solution to one problem with the fundraiser Madison had still been worrying about.

"You offer sweets and a hot drink, and you'll get a lot of people interested." Brooke looked her over. "What are you up to?"

"You'll find out soon enough," Madison promised. She changed the topic. "Is this a busy time of year for you as well, Yvette?"

"I don't think there's a slow time of year as a veterinarian, to be honest," Yvette said.

Alex sauntered past, catching the last bit of the conversation. "The kitten chasing that you were doing in the barn today didn't seem too strenuous. Cute, but not very strenuous."

Yvette raised a brow. "Spying on me?"

"Working," Alex said back. "Always busy as a ranch hand, you know. With things bigger than kittens."

"Veterinarians work with *all* animals, because we're skilled that way," Yvette said dryly, turning her back on Alex. "I hope you were enjoying your time with the goats. Since that's your area of expertise. Or was it the donkeys today?"

Brooke snorted before covering her face with a hand.

Alex grinned good-naturedly. "Nothing wrong with being a kitten wrangler." He eyed Yvette up and down before walking away.

Madison tilted her head toward the cowboy. "What was that about?"

"He and Yvette have something going on, but none of us are sure what," Brooke shared. "They argue about everything from what kind of mac and cheese is best to making weird comments about kittens."

"He's just impossible," Yvette said. "And we do not have something going on."

Brooke was desperately trying not to smile. Once Yvette was busy again, she leaned in and quietly shared, "She does like him, but he keeps pushing the wrong buttons. At some point the two of them are going to go up like nitroglycerin. That's my bet."

"Why are you constantly making comments that involve explosions and/or fires?" Mack shuddered comically as he joined them.

"Because it's so much fun to tease you, honeybun," Brooke said sweetly before draping her arms around his neck, preparing to give him a kiss.

"Ouch." Mack stepped back quickly. "These sweaters were not meant for public displays of affection."

The boxes on the table were nearly empty, and the pile by the door was enormous. People pulled on their coats to load the full hampers into the trucks parked outside, then everybody came back in for a final drink and snack before leaving.

Ryan motioned them toward the now-empty tables. "We have hot chocolate and gingersnaps before you leave. Thank you, everyone, for taking the time to help us."

Madison caught his eye, and he nodded, gesturing her forward.

She offered a wave as the group settled, smiles falling on her as they took in her sweater. "Before you go, I have one last thing to share on behalf of the Heart Falls Hope Fund. While I'm visiting, Ryan has been generous enough to allow me to meddle in his life, which means possibly meddling in yours."

Laughter rippled across the room.

Madison glanced at her new friends in the room and found both Brooke and Yvette smiling, although with a great deal of curiosity on their faces.

"It's been pointed out this is a busy time of year, but it's also a great time for us to count our blessings and give a hand to people who need it. Just like you did tonight in helping put together the hampers, I hope you'll be interested in a fun way to get some money into the fund so we start this coming year off right."

"Aren't you supposed to be ringing bells if you're asking us for money?" Alex asked.

"I'll ring bells if you want, but we have an idea that will be even more fun and involve more people. If you're interested in helping, or are even mildly curious to find out exactly how embarrassing this potentially could be for people, put down your email. I'm getting the details together now, and I'll let you know as soon as everything's finalized. The one thing I can tell you is the event will be December twenty-first, starting at six p.m."

She held the paper she'd been waving in the air to Ryan, and he moved to pass it around the room, a pen along with it.

"This isn't going to require hard labour, is it?" someone asked.

"Nothing kinky, right?"

There were a few laughs, and a few more when somebody else added "nothing but kinky." That got them a smack with the back of a hand and a lot more giggles.

"You want details? You're so demanding," Madison said with a grin. "Think about someone you know and love up on the stage in front of all of Heart Falls—presenting their best 'How I Love Being a Cow' interpretive dance." A hearty laugh burst from the crowd. She raised a hand to hold off the rest of their questions. "I'm making this up as I go along. But I promise you will know *exactly* how much it will cost to embarrass your friends by Monday."

"Sounds promising." That was from Alex. He had an evil glint in his eyes as he focused across the room. Madison followed his gaze to discover he was watching Yvette.

Oh, boy. This was going to be interesting.

10

Not everyone who had come out to help with the hampers left. Some of them stuck around once the doors to the pub were officially open, dancing and drinking and enjoying each other's company.

They also talked up the fundraiser, and in the end, Ryan posted sign-up sheets in multiple places around the bar. Curiosity was rising, and there were a lot of grins as he and Madison stayed working until midnight.

"Don't bother coming in the morning," Grace told him. She waved off his protest. "I've been working through the inventory; I'll put in the orders for this coming week. I plan on asking for a vacation in January, so let me butter you up now so that you can't say no."

"You're a treasure," Ryan assured her. "We'll figure out your vacation time. But for now, it's nice to have extra time with Madison."

"That's what I figured," Grace said with a smile. She waved at Madison. "Thank you. It was good to have your help behind the counter."

The crowd moved forward, hands raised as some shouted out orders.

Ryan took Madison by the hand and pulled her away before they could both end up back in the thick of things.

Madison breathed out a huge sigh as she relaxed back into the truck seat. "I love the excitement of working in a bar, but it does get loud. It's so nice to just be able to have quiet."

"You're good around people," Ryan told her. "I mean, I knew that, but I had kind of forgotten exactly how much of a Pied Piper you are. Only with people, not rats."

"Oh, goody. I'm the real Pied Piper who creepily lured all the children away." Madison twisted her head and smiled tiredly. "We should just sleep on this and let you come up with a new metaphor in the morning."

The great idea of the morning was an invitation to join his friends at Buns and Roses. Late morning, thank goodness. They both slept in again, making it over to the café for the ten o'clock meetup with only minutes to spare.

"Mack and I are treating you all," Brooke said, catching Madison by the hand before she could settle in a chair. "But the ladies get to decide what we're eating. Come on."

It was amusing to see Madison slip an arm through Yvette's, tucked in close as they examined the menu on the wall.

"So." Alex leaned toward Ryan.

Ryan waited, but Alex didn't do anything except bounce his gaze between Ryan and where Madison stood laughing with the other women.

Oh. Oh, *no*. The whole thing about being unexpectedly attracted to Madison was not a topic that would be discussed with anyone.

Ryan made sure to keep his expression blank. "Did you have a question, or have you developed a visual tick we need to get checked?"

"Just wondering how the reunion is going." Alex raised his brows. Repetitively. Wait—he was *waggling* them.

Good grief. "We're just friends," Ryan insisted.

Alex dipped his chin. "Anything you say."

"You're such a jerk," Mack muttered, leaning back so far in his chair, Ryan thought he'd tip over.

Ryan followed the man's line of sight to discover Mack was staring at his wife's hips as she stood at the counter. "Stop drooling." Ryan smacked his friend on the arm. "And stop gloating. The gloating is really beneath you."

"That's not what was beneath me this morning," Mack said softly, a contented sigh escaping as he eyed Brooke. A second later both Ryan and Alex pelted him with their gloves, and Mack raised his hands with a laugh. "Hey. Can't help pointing out my fantastic good sense of finding a wonderful woman."

"You can help it. Try," Alex warned. He leaned forward. "Also, next time you tell me to come for breakfast, I want a heads-up if you're also inviting that woman."

Mack looked confused for a moment. "Yvette?"

Alex made a face. Glanced over at Ryan. Glanced up to make sure the ladies were still at the counter before he leaned in and lowered his voice. "She's mad about me."

"I'm pretty sure she's mad *at* you," Mack corrected. "I think that's what Brooke told me."

Ryan wiped at his mouth and tried to hide his amusement.

Alex shook his head in disgust. "And you still asked me to come for breakfast with her?"

Mack shrugged. "I like your company. Not quite sure why at this moment, but anyway. Brooke likes Yvette's. Get over it."

"She constantly contradicts me," Alex complained.

Ryan thought about it for a moment then shook his head. "Actually, I think you kind of do that to her."

"Maybe you do it to each other," Mack suggested. He

lowered his voice warningly. "Just don't do it while we're eating breakfast. Simple. Be nice."

The last came out as a sharp order. Alex shook his head but offered an exaggerated sigh. "I will be a paragon of virtue," he promised.

At the table behind them, Ryan spotted Sonora Fallen. The older woman, grandmother to Tansy and Rose, was contentedly sipping coffee while she nibbled on a muffin and read something on her phone.

A comfortable Sunday morning out. Ryan smiled. He'd have to introduce Madison to the woman who was also in charge of the local pet rescue.

It took a moment before Ryan realized that the older man sitting with his back to Sonora was none other than Ashton Stewart. Ryan hesitated before calling out a greeting.

Ashton had to know they were there. The arrival of their group of six—including Ryan, Mack, and Alex—had not been quiet enough to overlook. There had to be some reason that the other volunteer supervisor from the fire hall hadn't at least offered a good morning. Instead, he stared resolutely at his plate, cutting into his breakfast and quietly gazing off into space between bites.

Before Ryan could decide what to do, the girls returned with the first round of food and drinks. Madison settled beside him, Yvette beside her. Which meant the six of them in a circle with the three men on one side of the table, the three women on the other.

At least that kept Alex and Yvette apart so they couldn't do childish things like stick forks into each other.

"Bacon and cheese quiches, cream cheese pumpkin muffins, gingersnap something or other," Yvette said, pointing to each item. "And there are cinnamon buns coming later. Tansy says ten minutes and a fresh batch will be out of the oven."

Everyone helped themselves. Even Alex didn't seem to have anything to complain about the choices before him.

Mack asked Alex something about changes at the Silver Stone ranch, but Ryan was more interested in eavesdropping on the girls. Especially when Yvette started with the question he'd been meaning to ask Madison all along but for some reason had continued to miss it.

"Brooke said you're heading to a new job. Leaving behind any broken hearts?" Yvette asked.

Madison choked for a moment, before apologizing with a laugh. "No boyfriends or girlfriends. No romantic entanglements whatsoever."

Brooke frowned. "Not interested?"

"No time," Madison shared, snagging one of the pumpkin muffins and spreading the cream cheese icing over the side. She glanced up and continued quietly, "I've been helping take care of my little brothers since my dad died. Not a lot of guys want to date someone who has two twelve-year-olds to do homework with and take to sports practice."

"Damn. That must've been tough." Brooke's expression didn't lighten. "You were chatting with your brother the other day."

"They're eighteen now, so they just needed a guiding hand." Madison looked a little uncomfortable. "They're good kids. I'm really happy I got to make a difference."

Considering how little she talked about herself, this had to be awkward. Ryan twisted to the side, slipping his hand around her waist and giving her a squeeze. "You okay?"

She dipped her head and offered a smile. "Of course. I keep forgetting that what's normal to me is kind of not normal. You might have to reassure your friends that I'm all right."

He reached up and tapped her nose. "Don't kid yourself, Maddy. Your life is *not* normal, but it suits you. You're a rock star."

That got a snort out of her.

"Please." She fixed her gaze on Alex, who had just finished making a laughing comment to Mack. "Alex. I was told I might be able to go for a horse ride while I was here. Is that something I should talk to you about?"

"If you're setting up rides, I want to come," Brooke said, raising her hand in the air and shaking her fingers eagerly.

"Me too," Yvette said before making a face. "Damn, I can't believe I just said that. I'm going to owe you one, Alex."

Alex grinned. "Always good to have a pretty girl owing me a ride."

The silence that fell instantly was deafening. Ryan was shocked and displeased. His friend was not usually an asshole. "Alex. I can't believe you just said that."

"I can't believe you said that moments after my *wife* asked for a favour." Mack folded his arms over his massive chest and looked very disapproving.

Alex tilted his head to stare at the ceiling, his tan skin flushed. "Well, that's kind of not what I meant. Damn."

For a moment, Ryan wasn't sure what the women would respond with when suddenly, Yvette laughed. "Are you *blushing*?"

Alex was. He definitely was.

"That was more trouble than it's worth." This comment from an unexpected source. Sonora stood at the side of their table staring disapprovingly at Alex. She turned her gaze on the three women sitting with Ryan. Crinkles formed at the side of her eyes as she smiled and held out a hand to Madison. "Sonora Fallen. If you three would like to go for a ride, I can make that happen."

Madison grinned. "That's wonderful. Thank you."

Yvette was still peering at Alex in wonder, but she answered Sonora as well. "That is great. Both the going for a ride and the fact that Alex feels about *this* big right now."

She held up a hand with her finger and thumb barely separated.

He met her gaze, his lips now curled into a rueful smile. "I apologize. I had about three smart-ass comments that wanted to come out at once, and they tangled together in a bad way."

"Then maybe you should try avoiding smart-assery," Yvette suggested smoothly. She turned back to Sonora. "Let's set up a time that works for everyone."

Conversation moved on, but Ryan noticed that Alex kept watching Yvette with something more than simple embarrassment as the meal finished up.

Madison leaned against Ryan. "Hard to eat with a boot in your mouth," she noted. "Yvette's not mad. If you want to assure your friend of that before he hurts himself trying to untangle this mess."

"Maybe he deserves to have to work to untangle it," Ryan whispered back.

But when the opportunity rose, he followed her lead and passed on the comment, feeling a little like they were back in middle school, passing notes with *do you like me, yes or no* on them.

Time with Madison was never boring.

THEY MADE it back to the house shortly after noon. Madison was glowing from the time spent with good people.

Even Alex. Poor guy. He should have stuck with "save a horse, ride a cowboy." That at least had tradition behind it.

"You've got good friends," she told Ryan as they slid into the living room, and she collapsed on the couch. Propping her feet up on the coffee table, she undid the button on her jeans and gave herself a little more room. "And you've got way too much good food happening for me. Excuse me. It's either this, or I'm gonna go put on my slouchy sweats."

"My home is yours," Ryan told her. He sat in the chair beside her, leaning back slightly and groaning. "I shouldn't have had that last cinnamon bun."

"What? You mean four was too many? Aww, poor baby."

"Shut up," he told her with a grin. Then his expression went serious. "I'm sorry the topic of your brothers came up."

She hesitated. "What part of it?"

He looked confused.

"What part are you sorry about?" she asked. "Because it's not a problem. Really."

No longer relaxed, Ryan stepped forward. "Madison. You don't ever complain, and I can admire that. But you having to quit school and go home to help raise your brothers is not something that most twenty-year-olds would do."

"So?"

"So it's okay for you to—" He stalled. Looked confused.

Madison stretched her arms over her head, twinging a little at one of the remaining bruises on her ribs. "Yeah, *that*. See, when I mention things like I quit school to go home and help raise my brothers, people assume I'm heading one of two ways. Either I want sympathy, or I want cookies. But Ryan?" She met his gaze. "I don't need either of those things. Dad died, and mom got broken for a while. They're my family, and they needed me. That's all there is to it."

He was on his feet, pacing.

They both stayed silent, Madison because she'd said everything she needed to say, and Ryan because—

Maybe he was dealing with his own baggage. She wasn't going to assume.

When he stopped abruptly and sat on the couch next to her, there was moisture in his eyes.

"I need a hug." He said it softly. Reluctantly even.

She opened her arms.

A moment later he'd hauled her against him, wiggling until they were side by side and she was resting against him with one hand over his heart. Tangled together just enough that it was the laziest hug ever, and yet precious and perfect.

Her ear rested on his shoulder, and under her palm, his heartbeat slowed. Evened out. She patted him gently. "We're just two people trying to get this right. Trying to do *what's* right with the hand we've been dealt."

"I don't like what I've been dealt," Ryan whispered against her hair. "I think that, and then I want to slap some sense into myself. Because even though my time with Justina was short, it was precious. It gave me Talia. How can I wish that away?"

"I get it. Oh, boy, do I get it." Madison was shocked to find her voice shaking. "If my dad hadn't died, my world would've been so different. I would've finished college with you. Who knows what I would be doing for work right now?"

Ryan ran his fingers through her hair, petting her. Quieting her.

This was one chance in a million for her to actually say these things, because he was the only person she could talk to about this.

She took a breath. "If my mom hadn't had a breakdown, my world would've been different. I could've gone back to school. I might've had a boyfriend. Maybe I would've fallen in love."

They were all the *what if's* she had dreamed about in the tough moments, but every time, she went back to the one truth she refused to let go of.

Madison tilted her head back until she met Ryan's gaze. "Instead of those worlds, I have this one. I have the joy of knowing my mom is pretty much one hundred percent again. I have two brothers who in that original alternate universe I probably wouldn't even know because I would've been gone. With the difference in our ages, I would've been off doing grown-up stuff instead of helping with first days of school, packing lunches, and teaching them to ride bikes. And while it's an odd thing to say because I can't change the past, I *wouldn't* change it knowing where we've landed."

Ryan was nodding slowly, considering.

Madison tapped his chest for a moment then wiggled away, heading to the kitchen to grab a tissue so she could wipe at her eyes and blow her nose. Great conversations that left you a watery mess needed to come with a warning label to have cleanup close by.

She smiled as Ryan grabbed a tissue himself.

They stood there in the kitchen, taking deep breaths and pulling themselves back together.

"I'm glad you have Talia and all these great friends. I am really happy for you," Madison said honestly.

Ryan dipped his chin, gazing somewhere near their feet. "I was angry for you sometimes," he admitted. "That you were off taking care of your brothers instead of getting to live your life."

"But it *was* my life," Madison pointed out. "There're a lot of people in this world doing ordinary things because it's the right thing to do. Like you, raising Talia on your own. Taking her to ballet class. Making sure she had a tutu."

"A *pink* tutu," Ryan clarified.

Just the way he said it made Madison laugh. She could picture Talia, hear her voice as she insisted on the colour. She could see Ryan patiently making sure that it happened.

Madison caught hold of his hand and held it between them. "And all those ordinary things line up to be something extraordinary when it comes down to it. Ryan, none of us are trying to be heroes. We're just trying to be happy and keep our families growing. One day at a time."

He brushed his knuckles against her cheek. Wiping away another tear that had fallen. "You're very smart for a university dropout."

She inhaled sharply, a laugh and a reset. "You're very smart for a bartender."

They stood there, the truth of the past moments tangling them together hard and fast, just like their friendship had started so many years ago.

Something changed. Turned, like a key in the lock.

They stared at each other, only inches away. Madison felt the heat pouring off his body. Even without contact, he affected her.

She couldn't move.

She had to move. If she stayed here, she was going to do something she'd regret.

Ryan's fingers dropped to curl around her arm, squeezing before letting go. She took a deep breath, simultaneously disappointed and thankful that at least one of them hadn't completely lost track of reality.

But then his hands slid over her skin. Off her arm and onto her back. His big palm dropped to her lower back as his gaze stayed fixed on hers.

No wait. He was looking at her lips, and she couldn't breathe. Couldn't make her lungs expand farther than halfway, which was already too far because the pressure at her back had erased that inch between them.

The entire front of her torso and his made contact. Firm muscles pressed against her breasts, her abdomen, her hips. It seemed her nipples were equally eager to get into the action, tightening and pressing against the inside of her bra.

Mind whirling, vision spinning, Madison still thought maybe nothing would happen.

He caught her chin with his free hand, holding her immobile. "Say no if you don't want this."

Nothing registered except a dull pulse low in her core. "This?"

The fact he had her befuddled seemed to amuse him, and his lips curled upward. "A kiss, Madison. I'm going to kiss you."

His statement should've seemed dry or amusing, but the only thought echoing in her brain was simple. "Why on earth would I not want this?"

She wasn't sure who moved first, but his lips were on hers, she'd curled her arms around him, and they both dove in like a parched man after a drought.

Ryan slid the hand at her jaw around to cup the back of her head. He held her still as he deepened the kiss, nipping at her lower lip before teasing their tongues together.

A second later Madison found her back against the wall, pinned in place by his muscular body as the kiss went on and on. It was all teeth, lips, tongues, and gasping breaths, and it was so damn good.

She had no idea why it had taken so long for the two of them to finally take this step.

Fisting the fabric of his shirt, she jerked upright to pull it free from his jeans. The instant she had room, she pressed her palms against his heated skin, curling her fingers slightly to press her nails into him.

Ryan groaned into her mouth, adjusting his stance so one leg pressed between hers, making contact with her aching sex and drawing a gasp from her lips.

He didn't stop kissing her, but now his hips rocked, sending deliberate pressure against her clit through the layers of fabric dividing them. Madison curled her hands around to his back and down, sliding under the back edge of his jeans. Every time he flexed his hips, his ass muscles contracted under her fingertips.

Dear God, she wanted him naked so she could watch those muscles. She wanted to be the one naked so the connection between them would be even more intense. Skin on skin, teasing even as they took the pleasure to a whole new level.

Ryan's fingers tightened in the hair at the back of her head, pulling their lips apart. He was breathing so hard that each harsh exhale made the small hairs on either side of her face wave.

Lust and want and need painted his expression. Madison was pretty damn sure that everything on his face was reflected on her own.

She went to lean closer, wanting to continue. Craving another taste.

Something dark and confused flashed in his eyes. Ryan let go.

Not only that, he seemed to step away, not just physically, but a huge wall rose between them on another level as he dragged a hand through his hair and paced silently across the room. "*Fuck.*"

She was lost for words. She hadn't forced him. He hadn't forced her.

He'd asked, and she'd been—

Ryan grabbed a coat out of the front closet, jamming his feet into his boots. He didn't look at her. "I'm going to pick up Talia."

He was out the door a second later, cold air reaching icy fingers toward her in a ghostly caress, frigid against her heated skin.

Madison walked away, breathing still out of whack, pulse uncertain. For a few minutes, she couldn't do anything except work to keep vertical as she paced around the house.

For one beautiful moment, everything in her world had lined up. Kissing Ryan—being in his arms—hadn't just been the right thing but the *only* thing. It was as if there were no other possible paths to follow.

Then he'd walked away.

What the hell, Ryan?

She shook her head, chastising herself for the moment of

annoyance. She didn't really blame him. Not for this part. This part she knew. He hadn't walked away from her. He'd been attempting to escape from what he didn't understand. Trying to deal with the shock.

Heck, she was shocked as well. Didn't mean it shouldn't have happened.

Understanding came out of the blue, crystal-clear. She stopped in her tracks and clutched the back of the kitchen chair beside her. The pure revelation gave her a solid place to stand, and as her heart and body settled back in something near normal, Madison breathed in fully for the first time in minutes.

She'd experienced this sensation before. That moment when something was absolutely right, when she'd known absolutely the thing that needed to be done in order to fix the problem.

This thing burning between her and Ryan—it wasn't wrong. The friendship they had, and what had pulled them together in the beginning, had been exactly what they'd needed then. Him falling in love with Justina had been right. It'd been exactly what he was supposed to do in that place and time, and that's why she'd never felt any jealousy.

But here? Now?

If she was going to make a list of the people Ryan should consider dating, there would be only one person on it.

Her.

She wandered through the house for a few minutes, cleaning up a little bit here, flipping through books there. The whole time, her mind raced.

Ryan had felt something. As her friend, though, he probably thought they shouldn't get involved. He assumed she was headed to some wonderful new start in Toronto where she would finally get to do everything she wanted instead of being stuck.

What if what she wanted was right here in Heart Falls with him?

It was what was best for her, she was sure of it. Best for Ryan? Oh, that was pretty certain as well. She'd loved him as a friend forever.

It would be a change of mindset to become more than friends, but she was sure they could work their way through that together. She just needed to let him know she was willing to change her plans in order to be with him. In order to stay with him and Talia.

So they could be a couple. Fall deeply in love.

Be a family.

She caught herself smiling, and the innocent expression of joy felt...

Sweet. Encouraging.

She had a lot of practice at the *family* thing, and it was something she truly loved. She'd never dreamed that what she'd done in the past might have laid the foundation for now.

Madison sat in a straight-backed chair at the small kitchen table and stared over the snowy fields, praying for wisdom to make the future she was dreaming of come true.

11

Ryan was well outside the town limits of Heart Falls before his heart rate dropped and his brain clicked back online.

He was smart enough to realize he'd fucked up in a million ways, not the least of which was leaving at high speed like a scared rabbit being chased by a dragon. What must Madison be thinking right now?

Although that was part of the problem. *Neither* of them had been thinking.

The moment of physical weakness had been brought on by the sharing they'd done. Ryan couldn't regret that part. Just the bit where he lost control afterward.

Dear God, Madison must be furious.

He shook his head.

Only…

Amongst the spinning information in his brain, one point slipped in hard. Madison had shared she hadn't had a boyfriend recently. Did that mean not once in ten years? Because, *fuck*.

Neither of them had been celibate during their high school

or college years. Teasing each other about their dates had been an amusing pastime, at least until he'd been introduced to Justina, and then Madison teased him about how hard and fast he'd fallen.

There wasn't anything funny about not having been intimate with someone for a long period of time. Ryan knew.

His thoughts warped, sliding into his first memory of Justina. It'd been early December, and Madison had not only hit him with the ugly sweater debacle, she'd waited until he'd worn it for the first time before making her move. She'd sneakily arranged a meeting between him and this woman she'd just *happened* to be doing a group project with. This woman she just happened to think Ryan would be into.

That day, meeting Justina's gaze, Ryan felt as if he'd smacked into a wall. She was petite, beautiful, sunshine in her laughter—and she'd looked at him as if she felt just as gobsmacked. Just as tangled up in falling into him.

Up until then, if anyone had mentioned love at first sight, Ryan would've totally laughed and said that was something for fairy tales.

Then he'd felt it. Experienced it. Considering he and Justina were engaged in under a month, falling in love had been one of the simplest and most perfect things in Ryan's life.

If he were being truthful, what he felt right now for Madison wasn't the same as that magical moment with Justina. He had all sorts of memories and emotions tied up in the time he and Madison had spent together over the years. Heck, he would even say he did love her, but he wasn't *in love* with her. The two sensations were nothing alike.

But the fact that he cared about her, that he wanted to do things to make her happy, those were things that a good friend—

No, he was just a fucked-up bastard, because he was trying to come up with a way to justify getting her into his bed. No matter how logical it was, no matter that they were both adults with physical needs, he shouldn't…

Still wanted to.

Oh, hell. If he hadn't been driving, Ryan would've laid his head on the steering wheel and closed his eyes.

He couldn't deny—it wasn't *only* lust he felt. Somehow the pulse of sexual need was tangled up in all the emotions he had from their years together. Still, Madison had plans that would be taking her away, so there was no use in worrying about anything beyond this holiday season.

But while she was there, while she was staying with him. Maybe they could—

If *she* wanted—

Ryan all but rolled his eyes at himself. He was a grown-ass adult, and there was no reason to try to sugarcoat the words or deny them. When he got back, he would straight-up ask if she was interested in getting involved for the duration of her stay. Give to each other, make each other happy.

Satisfy needs that had been denied for a long, long time.

The images that came to mind were not ones he wanted to deal with while driving down a remote section of highway. Picturing Madison close enough to touch, slipping off that soft, slouchy top she'd worn the other day. Helping peel the yoga pants down her legs, caressing and teasing every bit of skin that he bared.

He wanted to strip off her neon socks and kiss her toes, which just proved exactly how far gone he was at the moment.

Now he had to hope he hadn't messed up too much when he'd sprinted from the room.

Pulling in the car in front of his parents' home meant taking a deep breath and a mental reset. He had a lot of things to still line up today. Sweet-talking Madison into his bed would have to come at the end of the list.

His daughter met him at the front door of the house. Talia

looked past him, her expression falling when she noticed he was alone. “Where’s Madison?”

“She’s relaxing at the house. We’ll see her soon enough,” Ryan reminded his daughter.

Pickup on Sunday afternoon was always a shorter visit with his parents. The best routine had been to time it so when Talia and he got home, they had most the afternoon still to prepare for the week ahead.

Ryan didn’t make the mistake of bringing up the birthday party on the drive. He wanted to have his full attention available when they discussed *that*.

Other than endless questions about Madison, which he mostly managed to answer, Talia wanted to talk about her friends and the upcoming ballet she was so excited about.

The instant they got home, she raced for the door, backpack swinging over her shoulder.

Ryan approached the entrance a little slower. Having made his decision about how to go about what should come next between him and Madison only answered part of his problem.

He still had to apologize to her for going off without an explanation.

Madison looked up from the couch as Talia threw herself forward. “Hey, Tornado Talia. Did you have a good time with your grandparents?”

“I did. You didn’t come to get me,” Talia complained.

“I had things to do here,” Madison said, her gaze flicking to Ryan’s. There was a bit of a cloud of concern there, a little less of that lighthearted, full-of-joy look he expected from his friend.

As if she were being cautious, worried about him going off again. Yeah, he’d blown it big time, but now that the idea had been planted, he was pretty sure he’d be able to turn things around.

Once they had time alone.

That hard pulse struck inside again, but this time accompanied by a sense of anticipation. Ryan caught himself smiling slightly as he turned to his daughter.

"Now we have things to do," Ryan reminded Talia. He looked up and included Madison in his comment. "Maybe Madison can help us get ready for this week."

As expected, Madison rose to her feet and came forward, lips curled upward. Her smile was real. "Sure. What're we doing?"

The next half hour was full of preparing school lunch boxes and clothes prep—the bits that could be done ahead of time so that mornings weren't as chaotic. After that, Ryan sat down with Talia to make sure all her homework was finished.

Only once all that was done did Ryan dare to approach the topic of Talia's birthday.

He sat in his chair and pulled his daughter onto his knee. "We need to figure something out, and you have me a little mixed up. So, let's get everything unmixed up, okay?"

Talia tilted her head and waited.

"Your birthday is on December twenty-fifth," Ryan began.

She didn't break eye contact. "Yes."

For once, she had nothing more to say. Massively unhelpful.

Ryan proceeded cautiously. "Usually we have a birthday party early, so that your friends can come."

His sweet little girl folded her arms over her chest, staring out the window.

Yeah, that wasn't an answer. "You said something about not wanting to do that this year. Which is up to you, but what *do* you want to do to make your birthday special?"

She opened and closed her mouth a couple of times, and then a rush of words poured out of her. "I want to celebrate my birthday on my *birthday*. It's really important. Since I know Santa Claus isn't real, I don't need presents from him. I mean, I like presents, but I want them to be for my birthday, because *that's* what's real. And I know some people have Christmas by going to church, but we don't, and it's not even Jesus's *real* birthday. He was born in the summertime."

A small noise escaped Madison. She choked it off before Ryan could figure out if she'd strangled a laugh or gasp.

Knowing Madison? His daughter's blunt-spoken truth would've amused more than shocked her. He met Madison's gaze. It was clear she was asking for permission before joining in.

He'd welcome her help, but first, he had an idea of where to start. "We can celebrate your birthday on the twenty-fifth, but it might mean not getting to include your friends. I want you to have the special celebration you pick, but I don't want you to be sad without friends."

"You'll be there." Talia twisted toward Madison. "You'll still be here for my birthday, won't you?"

"If you want me to be. I would be honoured to celebrate your natal day," Madison said solemnly. "Can I ask a question, though? Did learning something about traditions from around the world make you want to change what happens this year?"

Talia's eyes went wide as saucers, as if Madison were magical to have spoken those words.

Frankly, Ryan thought Madison *was* pretty much a wizard to have come up with that out of seemingly nowhere.

"It's bad luck to celebrate your birthday on the wrong day," Talia insisted.

"Some cultures believe that, yes," Madison agreed. "But some also don't celebrate the day they're born but on a single day that's like a birthday party for everyone. Did you hear about that tradition?"

Talia shook her head slowly.

Madison spoke slowly, leaning forward on her elbows as she sat on the couch. "The most important thing you can do is think about what's right for you *and* your friends. Which means keeping the parts of traditions where the good memories live."

"Like the ugly sweater you and Daddy share?" Talia was no longer holding herself tight like a statue but leaning against him. Listening intently to Madison.

"Exactly. That's a good tradition for us, so we've kept it. The special show where you're going to dance? *That's* not going to be traditional, because we're changing to make it right for Heart Falls. All so it's easier to make others happy. And make ourselves happy in the process."

"So I can still have a birthday party?" Talia asked, seeming confused.

"You can have a birthday party," Ryan assured her, "but it might not be on your birthday. Missing *their* Christmas celebrations would make your friends unhappy."

Talia laid her head against his chest. "I don't know what to do."

"We don't have to decide right now. In fact, let's not make a decision for a few days. Let's talk about it more. Also, Madison and I will see if we can come up with some different ideas. Different options for you to think about. Will that help?"

She nodded. "Thank you, Daddy."

He pressed a kiss to her forehead. "I love you, little one. We'll figure it out."

Talia slipped off his lap, racing across to Madison. Throwing herself into her arms and squeezing her tight. "Thank you, Maddy."

Madison's face was unreadable in that moment. She wrapped her arms around his daughter and returned the tight embrace. "You're very welcome. And your daddy's smart. We'll figure something out that's a celebration, and fun, and just right for you."

~

TIME TICKED PAST SLOWLY. Every move Ryan made had Madison twitching like a cautious mouse looking for a safe place to hide.

Dealing with Talia's concerns over her birthday party had actually been a relief. Madison was confident they'd not only be able to solve it but make it into something amazing—ideas were already whirling through her brain.

But that was a few hours ago, and now all of her attention came to pointed peak.

Once Talia was tucked into bed, Ryan moved toward Madison. Determination in his eyes but with a slow, deliberate gait, as if worried he'd spook her.

Which was funny. She knew exactly what she wanted, but actually telling him—

Nope. Couldn't find the words. Her, who had once walked the entire length of a school corridor with Ryan using her as a boner block so the rest of the class couldn't see that he had a hard-on.

Gah. Thinking about *Ryan* and *hard-ons* just made it worse.

"Madison." She glanced up to find he'd stopped one pace away. "We need to talk."

Oh, boy.

He took her by the hand and tugged her toward the couch. The next thing she knew, they were seated together, thighs touching. Close enough that when he stretched his arm out along the back of the couch, her body swayed toward him.

Instinctively, or pushed by some part of her brain she had no control over, Madison lifted a hand to his cheek. Her palm brushed the faint five o'clock scruff on his skin.

If she hadn't been so close, if she hadn't been watching so intently, she would've missed it. The slightest of shivers, the flare of desire in his eyes.

When he lifted his free hand and pressed it over hers, tension inside grew.

Ryan took her hand, pressed his lips to her palm. A kiss, sweet and gentle.

Hot enough Madison was ready to self-ignite.

"I'm sorry for running out on you this afternoon," he whispered.

"Thank God you didn't just apologize for kissing me," Madison said somewhere between an attempt to ease the tension and blurting out the sheer, honest truth.

He tilted his head. "Not about to apologize for doing what I truly wanted."

He kissed her palm again, then each of her fingertips. When he moved her hand so his lips found her wrist, Madison wasn't breathing so smoothly anymore.

He lowered her hand to his thigh. Suddenly their mouths were only inches apart. Lips close enough, she was breathing his air. "*Ryan*."

"I'm not going to walk away again," he said.

Worked for her. "Good."

She closed the final distance.

Unlike earlier in the afternoon, the kiss started slow and stayed that way. A treat for all her senses, it included Ryan's scent sliding into her, setting her nerves tingling. A deliberate taste this time—and one to be savoured.

His tongue teased the seam of her lips, and she opened. Tiny dips of his tongue through her lips followed, as if he were sipping expensive liquor and didn't want to waste it or rush the experience.

Under her fingers, his thigh had gone rigid. She allowed herself to touch. Caress. She let her hand drift higher, sliding over his hip as she settled just that little bit closer.

He groaned, and the sound sent a shiver through her. She was aching, the soft flutter low in her belly becoming a consistent drumbeat.

As good as this was, Madison was still aware of where they

were. Of how much they still needed to say to each other, no matter how right kissing Ryan was.

She slid her other hand up to his chest, just enough pressure to break the contact between their lips.

His pupils were huge as he stared over her face. "We need to talk, right?"

She nodded, amusement slipping in. "And this shouldn't happen here. Talia."

From his quick change of expression, Ryan had absolutely forgotten the possibility of his daughter walking in on them. Which said something amazing about exactly how into the kiss he'd been, but still—*no*.

He sat back, fingers tangling with hers as he rested them in his lap. "I realized something on the drive to pick up Talia. I think the two of us are both looking for something. I'll stop if you want me to, but I hope you don't."

Straight-up facts were necessary. "I want you," Madison confessed.

He closed his eyes, that shiver racing over him again. "*Fuck*."

"That's blunt." Madison let her fingers drift over his. Circling the back of his hand with her fingertips. Up his forearm. Those sexy, muscular arms that she been ogling the other day. The day before.

And a whole lot of days before that as well, if she were honest.

Ryan leaned in and brushed his cheek against hers. Pulled back in a scruff-roughened caress then kissed her again, still soft and gentle. "I want you. Not just because I'm craving a touch, because I want to touch *you*. I want to put a smile on your face, Maddy. I want my fingers on your skin, to tease and stroke until you feel light-headed and are swimming in pleasure. I want to taste you until you're so satisfied, you walk out of my house with an even bigger smile on your face than usual."

"Not a bad offer, hotshot." Madison glanced toward the hallway to where the bedrooms were. "But, careful."

"Yes. We'll be careful," he promised.

They were on their feet, fingers still meshed. When Ryan would've led her into her bedroom, she tilted her head toward his room.

They were inside, the door closed and locked behind them, before Ryan turned toward her, a wry smile on his face. "Can I say again how glad I am that you've ordered me a bigger bed?"

Her lips twitched. "Gee, assumption much?"

She covered her mouth to stop the squeal that nearly escaped as he picked her up and carried her toward his twin bed. Amusement danced in his eyes. "No assumptions about how far or how fast, but I said I was going to make you feel good. I can do that on *this* mattress, no problem."

"Let's hit the shower, instead," Madison suggested. She had an ulterior motive. Getting to see Ryan in all his naked glory wasn't something she wanted to delay gratification on.

He willingly changed directions, taking them into the bathroom. Reaching in to turn on the water in the shower before joining her beside the double-sink vanity.

When Madison would've stripped away her layers, Ryan caught her by the wrists. "My job. I like unwrapping presents."

"Good to know." The words came out a little breathless because he'd already closed the distance between them and slid his hands beneath her T-shirt. Warm palms inched up her back.

Madison couldn't help it. She closed her eyes and savoured the sensation. His mouth was back on hers, kissing softly, nipping at her lower lip before sucking gently. The entire time, his hands moved over her body. He undid her bra then reached down and caught hold of the fabric of her shirt before slowly peeling it over her head.

Her undone bra flopped awkwardly once the T-shirt was

gone, the neon-yellow cups and straps hanging over her skin but no longer lined up to support or hide any boob-like features.

"Sweet hell. *Bright* things? I thought we were talking about your socks, Mad, not your underwear." Ryan's smile faded slightly as he stripped away the bra, and his fingers lingered over the faint purple and green marks on her body. "Do they still hurt?"

"Terribly," she lied. When his gaze snapped up to hers, she stuck out her bottom lip just the slightest bit. "You should kiss them all better."

He didn't need any further encouragement. And now she was regretting the whole suggestion of shower time, because it meant she had to use muscles to remain vertical as he put his mouth on her.

He pressed kisses along her collarbone, gently caressing his fingers over her breasts. The expression on his face—

Priceless.

"I always knew my best friend had breasts, but I had no idea they were this sweet." Ryan stroked his thumbs against the sensitive underside, and goose bumps rose. Any remaining cold vanished as he leaned in and licked her skin. Teasing and touching and taking his time in endless circles before reaching the peak where she wanted him. Needed him.

Madison caught hold of his T-shirt, jerking it out of his jeans. Desperate to get him equally naked.

He must've sensed her frustration was no longer the fun type, because he stopped what he was doing for long enough to reach up over his head, grab his shirt, and jerk it forward. She caught the barest flash of a beautiful set of six-pack muscles before he reached for her. Sliding his thumbs under the elastic of her yoga pants, he pushed them down over her hips, pausing with his palms cradling her butt for a brief moment.

Slow was overrated. Madison undid his button and zipper,

shoving at his jeans and underwear. Somehow, between the two of them, the clothing was in a pile on the floor and Ryan had pulled her into the steamy shower.

It was big enough so they could stand apart and enjoy the view. The steam grew thicker, but she could still see enough to take in his trim hips and muscular legs. The way the water droplets flying off her body clung to him, turning his forearms into glistening masterpieces.

Ryan stepped in and pulled her against him before she was done admiring. Instead of her eyes, she used her hands. Stroking down his sides, teasing the Adonis muscles as they guided her down toward his rigid cock now pressed against her hip.

Their lips were back in contact, the kisses growing needier. It wasn't awkward, no matter how wet and even rough he got as they both began to lose control. Ryan tweaked her nipple then rapidly slid his hand down the side of her body until he cupped her possessively. Madison gasped as he pulsed his fingertips against her folds, slipping easily inside her wetness as her body welcomed him in.

One slightly adjusted stance, and they were both able to reach. Both able to tease—to take and give what they wanted.

Madison curled her fingers around his length, gentle as she explored, sliding the slick skin over his hard length. Ryan's head fell back, and he breathed out, a long, low sound that said *finally* as clearly as if he'd used words.

Madison tightened her fingers, sliding with the help of the water over him. Taking him up, teasing as she adjusted pressure.

She gasped as he got his concentration back enough to slide two fingers carefully into her, the heel of his palm centered over her clit.

He kissed her briefly, smiling. "I've got about five seconds left once you kick into gear. So first, let me play."

"Gentleman to the core," Madison said.

That grin flashed, and then he was on his knees, and it wasn't his palm on her clit, but his tongue. Fingers stroking inside her as if he planned to be there all day.

Which was a nice sentiment but totally unnecessary. She was maybe not quite five seconds away, but very, very close.

She stroked the hair off his forehead, the sheer beauty of watching her best friend give to her in this new yet ancient way—

The steady beat of his tongue, the steady pulse of his fingers. Those things brought her close, but it was the smile on his face, the fact that it was *him* touching her so intimately that sent her over the edge. Her body tightened around his fingers, tiny muscles pulsing.

"*Ryan.*" She breathed it out, the emotion coming from her soul. From somewhere deep, deep inside.

Sexual pleasure rolled through her system with all the ensuing happy endorphins. That had not sucked.

Well, okay, bad choice of words.

Her legs shook, but she was very much laughing with gentle amusement as Ryan rose to his feet, wrapped his arms around her, and pulled her against his body. Madison savoured that as well. The muscles under her fingers, the way his chest rocked. Especially when she tangled her fingers around his rigid cock.

He caught hold of her hair and turned her face up to him. This kiss wasn't as gentle, and as he took her lips, she tightened her grip. Pumped a little harder, and an instant later Ryan pulled back and swore. Hips pulsing erratically as he shot over her fingers, against her belly. His seed coating her as the water poured down on them both.

He leaned against the wall, pulling her over him. An instant later he'd angled the showerhead to keep them under the spray.

Then he held her until their breathing had begun to calm and their hearts were no longer racing.

Well. The entire adventure had been slightly unexpected, but pretty much everything she'd hoped for. She hadn't even had to talk him into it.

Madison rested her head against Ryan's chest. And dreamed.

12

It took a lot of effort the next day for Ryan to not grin like a banshee, headed out in public to drop off Talia for school then to work his normal day shift at the pub.

Madison seemed to be better at hiding her reaction to their previous evening's activities.

Then again, Maddy was usually a lot happier in her outward appearance than him, so he wasn't sure what change he expected to see.

She'd said goodbye to Talia at the house and left before them, with an excuse of "things to do." One of which he knew was meeting up with Rose to get her approval on the fundraiser email before it went out.

Madison being busy was probably a good thing on many levels. If she'd have come to the fire hall with him, chances are he'd have been so distracted by wanting to kiss her, he'd have been useless.

Kiss, then touch, then...

He cursed as he walked into a wall, stubbing his baby toe hard enough, the damn thing pulsed.

Okay, he did want sex. He wanted to experience that as well as a myriad of other adventures with Madison. But he wouldn't rush to make it happen.

It would be good. He had zero doubts on that score, based on the way Madison had damn near read his mind and stroked and touched him so perfectly—

...and he was hard again. Ryan dropped his head into his hands and focused on taking deep breaths.

Thankfully, he had a lot of tasks to keep him busy around the hall. He cleaned and scrubbed, refilled emergency kits. Alex stopped by unexpectedly just before lunch, joining him and Mack as they paused for a midday break.

In the middle of telling a joke, Mack stalled out. "What's your problem?" he asked Alex.

Both Ryan and Alex looked up, slightly shocked by the rapid interruption. Ryan because he'd been once again distractedly daydreaming about the next time he'd be able to corner Madison and find privacy.

Alex because...

Ryan frowned. "You're right. Something's up."

"Oh, bullshit. Just because he says it, doesn't make it true," Alex growled.

"No, but the fact you've reorganized every item on the table including lining up the salt and pepper shakers with military precision instead of sprawling back in your chair like usual, grinning at us for being suckers about posture..." Ryan shrugged. "Spill the beans."

"If I take a leave of absence, can you get me back onto the roster?" Alex asked Mack before glancing at Ryan. "And I believe the phrase I usually use is *stick up your ass*."

Mack snorted before wiping at his mouth and offering a gentle shrug. "Shouldn't be a problem. How long do you need off?"

"That's it. I don't know." Alex made a face. "Family stuff. I might have to head home for a while. Silver Stone will let me go, but I'd hate to have to jump through a ton of hoops here. But I don't want to leave you in the lurch."

A knock sounded, knuckles rattling against the wall beside the door. Ashton Stewart stepped into view, his bright eyes taking in the gathering and landing on Ryan. "Just the man I wanted to see."

As Ashton walked forward, Mack laid a hand on Alex's arm. "I'll double-check, but it shouldn't be a problem."

Ashton grabbed a coffee before pulling out a chair and settling beside them. He looked Ryan in the eye. "That visitor of yours. She's a bundle of trouble."

Ryan blinked. "Madison? What'd she do this time?"

Which got a laugh out of the other men.

"Yeah, that last bit kind of confirms this is normal behaviour for her." Ashton waved his phone in the air. "I got an email. It appears someone out there in Heart Falls is willing to pony up money for me to cavort on stage like a goat."

Dear God. The email—Madison said she would go over it with Rose to get her approval and then start blasting the information around town.

The terrible thing was, suddenly Ryan could picture Ashton having to put on a pair of furry ears and kick up his heels. In fact…

"I would pay money to see that," Ryan agreed.

He dove into his email. Mack and Alex were doing the same.

Sure enough, the message from the Heart Falls Hope Foundation was right there in his inbox.

On December 21, the Heart Falls community will perform their own variation on The Nutcracker. *Never seen* The Nutcracker *before?*

Don't worry, our variation has been uniquely adapted to our location and needs.

In the best of Christmas traditions everywhere, this classic story will be performed by the multiple talents within our community. The star ballerinas will be the Heart Falls troop coached by Charity Gruzing.

We are also raising money for the Heart Falls Hope Fund, which is where you come in.

Be a volunteer or be a donator. Or both!

For every five dollars donated, you receive a vote. (Volunteer hours already performed and/or a commitment of future hours can be traded for votes as well.)

Cast your votes to select which role our volunteers should play.

For example, if you really want to see fire chief Bradly Ford perform on stage in [our unique variation of] the role of the Mouse King, he must have the highest total votes in the category.

The winning performers will be required to:

1: devise an appropriate costume. We suggest recycle, reuse in all cases, rather than renting. Donate the money instead.

2: choreograph your own maximum two-minute interpretive dance (solo or in a group) to the music you will be provided.

Please check this online doc for a real-time list of the current potential performers and the amount offered for them to perform that role. This is a fundraiser, so be generous and sneaky. You have one week to choose your dream cast for this epic event. All bids close at three p.m. on Sunday, December 13.

Cast will be announced Monday morning, which will give you one week to create your costumes and choreograph your dance. Performance will be Monday, December 21 at 6 p.m. at the Heart Falls Community Centre. Five-dollar entrance fee for adults is suggested but not required.

Remember this event is family-friendly, and also for the sheer entertainment of it. Talent is not required.

Enthusiasm and a good sense of humour are.

Ryan clicked over to the Google doc just as Mack let out a braying laugh. "Ashton, good for you. At least twenty-six people want to see you cavorting like a goat."

Ashton leaned back and folded his arms over his chest. "You'd think some would have a little more respect for a man's position."

This was damn amusing. "You think those are all workers at Silver Stone?"

"Look at that, twenty-seven," Mack updated.

Alex put his phone down on the table and attempted to look innocent.

Ashton glared at him.

Alex shrugged. "What can I say? The ranch email encouraging our participation arrived at the same time, and I'm all for team spirit."

Ryan met the older man's eyes. The question Madison had asked previously made Ryan double-check his answer had been accurate. "If you do end up being asked to dance like a goat, will you do it?"

"Of course I will," Ashton said. "I'm not some curmudgeon

with no holiday spirit. Heart Falls is my home, and it's for the good of the community."

Other than the fact he said the first part with a bit too much emphasis, Ryan agreed with the sentiment.

Mack and Ashton took off to do a specific schedule check. Alex stayed where he was across from Ryan, hands pressed to the table, his cocky attitude vanished. He seemed to be trying to figure out what to say.

He finally spit it out. "Am I really a dick when I talk with Yvette?"

If the other man wanted honesty? "You're childish around her. Kind of like little boys in grade school who poke the girls they like."

"Well, shit." Alex pulled a face. "That would be because I *do* like her."

"Since neither of you is ten years old, it's probably not a good way to get her to reciprocate. Just saying," Ryan offered.

The other man leaned back, his lazy sprawl returning. "Well, since I'll be leaving town soon anyway, not much use worrying about my past mistakes. I shouldn't start something I can't finish."

Which was exactly the same conclusion Ryan had come to.

He met Alex's gaze. "When are you leaving?"

"Not sure. It'll probably be pretty last-minute."

"But you're coming back?" Ryan asked.

"Damn straight. Got a great job at Silver Stone and good friends here at the hall." Alex nodded slowly. "Just have to wait on anything more."

Something uncomfortable rolled in Ryan's gut. He couldn't wait to get home to find a time and a place to resume the sexual exploration with Madison. But the truth remained. She was leaving.

This new thing between them really had nowhere to go. It wouldn't do to get his hopes up.

YVETTE PICKED MADISON UP. She and Brooke had flipped a coin to see which of them would drive, the sheer competitiveness of which made Madison laugh.

She understood better when they were seated three across the bench seat in Yvette's truck, Madison in the middle.

She leaned forward as Yvette turned off the main highway and started up what looked more like a goat trail. "That's the road?"

"Not the main road, but yes." Yvette pointed to the top of the ridge where fainter tracks vanished under hard-packed snow. "That's the back side of Sonora's property. Her house and the pet-rescue barn are right off the main road."

"You'll see why we're going this way in a minute." Brooke tapped Madison on the shoulder and pointed in a different direction. "But here's a view you should appreciate. That's Silver Stone. All that land, pretty much from where we are to where the horizon ends."

"Wow." For a city girl who had spent a lot of time living in a condo when her brothers were young, the expanse looked like an enormous patch of wilderness. "Please tell me this isn't a survivor-type activity where you're going to abandon me and discover if I'm still alive come the spring."

Brooke leaned forward and smiled at Yvette. "This girl has got one hell of an imagination."

"I kind of figured that out when I discovered she turned both the Nutcracker and Clara into rag dolls. Or maybe not that part, because that's semi-canon. But the dance of coffee and tea turned into chickens and horses? *That* takes some flights of fancy."

They paused at a gate in the barbed wire fence. Madison was glad to be in the middle seat when Brooke pushed open her door and waded out into the shin-deep snow.

"Ah. The plot thickens. That's why you wanted to drive," Maddy accused Yvette.

"Guilty. Although I also like driving this road," Yvette said.

"Still don't think this is a road," Madison muttered. Brooke waited until Yvette had driven through then closed the gate after them.

Two more gates and they were over the top of the hill and down into a neat little valley tucked away from the wind. There was also a really small barn or a really big shelter—Madison didn't know enough to tell the difference between the two.

A small group of horses, already saddled and ready to ride, were gathered at the wooden railing around the arena. Sonora sat comfortably on her own horse, just outside the shelter.

She waved them forward, dismounting to join them as they crowded out of Yvette's truck. "Two birds with one stone. My grandson-in-law said the old-timers needed a little attention."

A tall man with dark hair and a gentle smile tipped his hat in their direction. "Brooke. Yvette." He stepped forward and held out a hand to her. "And you are Madison. I'm Walker Stone. Welcome, and thank you."

"Nice to meet you, and what am I saying *you're welcome* to?"

He grinned as he glanced at his grandma. "I hear you're the one who set up the dance thing happening in a few weeks."

Sonora *tsked* at him. "Are you planning on meddling?"

Walker lowered his voice conspiratorially. "It's too good of an opportunity to resist. Plus, it's a good cause. What time does the bidding end, again?"

"Three p.m. Sunday, so if you're planning anything Machiavellian-style, time your assault accordingly," Madison encouraged. "And open your pocketbooks wide."

"Got that part all planned," Walker said with a smile before tilting his head toward the horses. "Come on. They're all eager to meet you."

What followed was a little bit of holiday perfection that

Madison hadn't expected. Even though she knew she was headed to a rural community, Ryan wasn't really involved in that part of it, so she hadn't expected to be able to enjoy time on horseback.

Walker introduced them to three old and steady horses he said were retirees. "But they've done a lot of good work over the years, so it's nice to take them out every now and then and let them stretch their legs."

Madison had a beautiful dark-brown horse that pushed his nose against her belly, making her laugh until she got a chance to present him with the carrot Walker had slipped her.

They took a practice turn or two around the arena before Walker led them out and down a trail that wound its way around the little protected valley.

Once the group reached a more level spot, he twisted then tipped his hat again. "I'll just be up ahead."

A few minutes later, he was far enough out front that the four women had all the privacy they could've wanted.

Sonora rocked rhythmically as the horse moved under her, Yvette by her side, Brooke and Madison directly behind them. "He's a good boy, my grandson-in-law."

"All your grandkids are wonderful," Brooke assured her. "Tansy is single-handedly trying to get everyone in town to go up at least one pant size this winter."

Madison put two and two together. "I didn't know Tansy was your granddaughter."

"I have four of them," Sonora said happily. "The oldest, Ivy, is married to that wonderful man up ahead. Tansy and Rose you know from their shop. My youngest is off gallivanting at art school. Fern will be back for the holidays, though. I do like it when all my chicks are within arm's reach."

The image of Sonora as a mother hen was very appropriate.

"Will she be back in time for *The Nutcracker*?" Yvette asked.

She twisted toward Madison. "If you need artwork done, she's the one to ask."

That was on the to-do list. "Not that I want to assume, but can you recruit her for me, Sonora? If she has time? We don't need a lot, but something more than my drawing skills would be helpful."

"Of course. I know she'd be delighted." Sonora's smile widened. "You know how when people are doing what they're supposed to do, it just makes them happier? That's my granddaughter and making art."

That philosophy sounded a little like what Madison was thinking in terms of her and Ryan. Being friends had always made them happy.

Being more—so far, it was working out well.

"I believe she's done as of the fifteenth, so I'll let her know to get in touch with you." Sonora leaned forward on the saddle horn and twisted, dipping her chin at Madison with approval as she slightly changed the topic. "I like that you're doing things up not too fancy. I like that you changed the performance to fit Heart Falls."

"I do as well," Brooke agreed. "It's also nice that you made it work for everyone, and all ages, to take part."

"I like that you combined it with the fundraiser." Yvette said it slowly, but when she twisted to look at Madison, it was to offer a big smile and a wink. "It definitely is more fun thinking of people we know and love being up on the stage."

"Anyone who is not being a curmudgeon will want to be involved," Sonora said firmly. "Although, personally, if I were going to be any of the barn animals, I would pick a cat."

"You would make a wonderful cat," Yvette assured her.

The topic changed to the upcoming weather and other possibilities for getting together while Madison was still in town. She didn't mention anything about possibly extending her stay.

Until she and Ryan had talked about it, she wasn't going to.

No pressure on him, no pressure on anyone. No matter that she felt it was right. Not just her and Ryan, but these women, this time. The fresh air and the blue sky and the old reliable horse happily swaying under her as they rode through the brisk December air.

13

It seemed to take forever for Talia to settle down for bed on Monday night. She'd been vibrating from excitement after Charity had confirmed the Not-So-Nutcracker performance in two weeks' time.

Once his little girl had finally said good night, Ryan and Madison started in the kitchen.

He pulled her into his arms, holding her first, just needing that one-on-one adult body contact. Kissing came next, and he wasn't about to rush it, because even in the short time they'd had, he discovered kissing Madison was one of his favourite things.

She had a way of placing her body so she leaned against him. Not as if trying to entice them to go faster, push further. Just wanting contact points, as many of them as possible, while their lips explored.

Her soft breasts against his body, thumbs tucked into the waistband of his jeans. Trusting him to keep her from falling flat on her face—which was a pretty big act of trust, considering there were moments his legs weren't too damn steady. And they were only kissing.

The squeak of a door—Talia's room—made them jerk apart and try to act innocent as his daughter came and got a glass of water.

The time ten minutes after that was because she needed to cuddle.

The third time Talia interrupted them, Madison was clearly fighting hard not to laugh. "Come on, kiddo. I'll tuck you in one final time and tell you a story about my brothers and the time they decided to keep pet rocks."

Ryan took himself off to bed rather than try and tempt fate again.

Tuesday night he'd been on the first of his twelve-hour night shifts. Madison showed up around eight o'clock.

She waved at the other volunteers before joining Ryan where he sat in the common room reading a book. She settled next to him, thigh making contact, but not so close that anyone would comment. "How goes it, Mr. Firefighter?"

"Quiet so far." Ryan glanced into the other part of the hall and back at Madison. Her deep-auburn hair hung over her shoulders, only the faintest indent where her winter toque had been. Her eyes sparkled, and she looked—

Edible.

"You coming here isn't a good idea," Ryan said softly. "Because all I can think of right now is hauling you into the shower room and stripping you down."

"Well, now." Madison pressed fingers to her chest as if she were a virginal maiden aunt, expression mock shock. "And here I came to tell you that you're the current top selection for our Not-So-Nutcracker rag doll—male."

He laughed, draped an arm around her shoulders, and pressed a friendly kiss to her cheek. "You are incredible."

He laughed even harder when he headed to the bunkhouse after she left and discovered somehow, before innocently waving goodbye, Maddy had snuck in and stuffed his pillow into the gaudy sweater then sat it on his bunk. A headless, holiday scarecrow he was now sworn to wear.

Wednesday's big adventure was the arrival of the bed Madison had ordered for him. Ryan would've been tempted to make use of it immediately. Having Madison in the house and not being able to touch her when and where and how he wanted was making him itch like he'd fallen into a vat of holly leaves.

Of course, the delivery truck didn't pull into his driveway until just before three p.m.

Madison waved him off. "I've got this. You grab Talia, and once she's home, this might all be organized."

Ryan leaned in, crowding Madison out of the way of the delivery men from Calgary who were bringing in headboards and box springs. If he happened to use his body to pin her in place for a moment, stealing a quick kiss, it was from the excitement of a brand-new household item.

Although that didn't explain him catching hold of her hands and using his hips to pin her to the wall. "I can't wait to test it with you."

Madison's eyes went huge. Good reaction.

His daughter also approved, but mostly because she thought the bouncing potential was pretty amazing.

Talia squealed. "So pretty, Daddy."

His daughter rushed forward and threw herself on the mattress, messing up the dark bedspread. Ryan followed slower, happiness welling up at the childish pleasure Talia got in sprawling on the huge surface.

Madison had done a great job on a task he'd put off for too many years. The headboard was simple but a mix of dark and light wood that coordinated well with the other bits of furniture he had. The sheets were deep blue, the quilt shades of royal blues with touches of white and black, and the whole thing looked cozy and comfortable.

He wanted to see her hair spread out over the sheets, auburn flashes against the dark. Her pale skin—

He met her gaze, and a heat that matched his own shone in her eyes.

Which made going to his *second* overnight shift that much harder. And of course, this would be the night they had to respond to three emergency callouts and, just before four a.m., a fire in the dumpster behind the downtown businesses.

He was barely aware of Madison greeting him at the door with the promise to take care of Talia and get her to school.

"Thanks." He thought he'd said it. Thought he'd given his daughter a quick squeeze and a kiss goodbye.

What he did remember was stumbling to the bathroom.

A quick hot shower removed the scent of smoke, but Ryan needed his rest this morning. He got boxers on before crawling under the covers, then his head hit the pillow, and with a sigh, he closed his eyes.

In five seconds—maybe sooner—it registered. The sheets smelled like Maddy. The citrus body cream she used. Her not-quite-but-almost floral shampoo.

She slept in my bed last night.

He was hard before the thought fully took root.

With a groan, he rolled to his back and stared at the ceiling. The position left him extended fully without his feet hanging over the end of the mattress or hands hitting the side wall because of the narrow width. Comfortable everywhere except for his cock.

The realization was faintly amusing.

Damn woman was mischief to her core. He'd have to find a way to get revenge.

But exhaustion won out, even over nerves that were fired up and eager to tease Madison in all the erotic ways he could come up with. He fell asleep with dirty plans drifting in his brain.

Woke to the sensation of the mattress dipping just slightly beside him.

The grogginess in his brain vanished instantly as a cool feminine body pressed against his side. A hand slid over his chest, fingers spread wide, and then Madison was leaning against him and kissing his neck.

Lips and teeth drifted along his jawline until she closed in on his mouth and kissed him.

Not fully awake, his hands still knew what to do. As their mouths connected and his tongue dipped between her lips, Ryan rolled toward her and slid a hand over her hip.

Found bare skin.

His heart rate was no longer sedate and leisurely. "You naked?"

"Maybe," she whispered.

How was that even a *maybe* type question? Ryan chose to explore rather than chastise her. His search was answered quickly and thoroughly when he kept moving, his body coming to rest between her thighs.

He pushed up on his elbows and stared down. Madison was pink cheeked, and the flush was the only thing she wore.

Her breasts rocked with each deep inhale, their red-tipped peaks begging for him to use his mouth. Her skin glowed softly, temptingly, all the way down to the red-tinted curls covering her mound.

Madison opened her legs a little wider, and he settled in firmer, his cock pressed to her hot core. He rocked his hips slightly, and the heat and welcoming moisture made him shake in anticipation.

"I'm really regretting my boxers right now," Ryan whispered before looking up to meet her eyes. "No jokes, though. Do you want this?"

"I want you." She said it simply. Honesty in the words,

coupled with the fact she lifted a condom in the air, made Ryan's heart pump hard and fast.

Then he took her, slowly. So slowly, he had to have used all his goodness for the entire year in that one shot.

Kisses for her lips as Madison stroked her fingers over his shoulders and threaded them through his hair over and over again.

Kisses down her body, pausing to taste and enjoy her breasts until she arched under him, nails digging into where she clutched his biceps.

Kisses over her belly, dipping his tongue briefly into the shallow hollow before using his teeth on the skin over her hip bone. His hands cradled her ass, the skin against his fingers begging for him to stroke there as well until she quivered.

But even more tempting was brushing his lips along the inside of her thigh. Kissing, nipping, drawing a sharp gasp from her as he licked his way back up to her center.

He used his thumbs and opened her. "Merry Christmas to me," he muttered before pressing the softest kiss possible to the most sensitive part of her.

"Ryan." She said his name like a warning, like a request. Feet planted against the brand-new mattress, she lifted her hips and chased his mouth. Reached down and tangled her fingers in his hair to tug him back to where she wanted him.

It was too easy to smile. In spite of the aching hardness in his cock that still needed to be addressed, this was fun and playful and exactly what he expected from a romp in bed with his best friend.

He slipped a finger in and out. Added a second, licking more firmly over her clit as he moved slowly inside her. When he curled his fingers slightly, her answering moan told him he'd hit the jackpot.

Ryan eased up just enough to meet her eyes. "Want to come before, during, or after I'm inside you?"

"Don't stop." Her face twisted with pleasure as he pressed in again, skimming his thumb over her clit.

Before it was. Fine by him. He was going to be sorely pressed to last longer than a minute, all things considered.

He went back to using his mouth, taking in her taste and the moans slipping from her lips. They were more delicious than the sweet ambrosia she'd made for the fire hall potluck because she was here, in his bed. Body tightening around his fingers as she gasped his name.

It had been years, so he was impressed by how fast he got the condom on. An instant later he was back between her thighs, the head of his cock lined up with her heat.

He lifted up, met her eyes, and pushed home.

"*Yes.*" She breathed it out, then her face contorted. Before he could worry, though, she lifted her legs and wrapped them around his hips. "Still coming."

The words were tight, pleasure filled.

Ryan didn't really need the update. The pressure enveloping him would've been sweet no matter what, but with those muscles quivering around him, he guessed that his *under a minute* estimate had just been cut in half. He pulled back and thrust forward.

She dug her heels into his ass and drove him deeper. Okay, now he had seconds left.

He mashed their fingers together, pressing her hands to the bed on either side of her head. Stared into her eyes as he thrust in, and again, before the next one broke him. He locked them together, grinding his hips against her to add pressure to her clit because she was still squeezing. Still gasping as her first orgasm, or a new one, rolled on.

His brain poured out of him in a rush of pleasure.

Somehow, when it was over, he collapsed beside her and not on top. And then he laughed when she shoved him to his back and muttered something about keeping the sheets clean.

The sensation started deep inside. He glanced over as Madison cracked open one eye. She lay beside him, both of them still panting, both of them, he assumed, still reeling from the aftereffects of one hell of an awesome ride.

His ears rang.

He felt fantastic.

"I think that was a very thorough christening of your new mattress." Madison got the words out although it took her a few breaths.

Ryan leaned in and kissed her slowly, gently, and with a whole lot of heart. Then he whispered, "That was a good start. Don't go anywhere. I'll be right back."

By Monday, Madison could honestly say Ryan's mattress was just the perfect amount of firmness and exactly the right amount of softness.

They'd been on it pretty much every opportunity they had, especially over the weekend while Talia had been at her grandparents'. Madison was sore from so much activity after a drought, but every twinge of discomfort was totally worth it.

Sex with Ryan was fun and physically satisfying. But the part that made Madison quiver was the fact he'd started touching her outside of the bedroom. Always careful to make sure Talia wasn't around, or any too-observant public witnesses, Ryan nevertheless stood close. Pressed a hand to her lower back. Brushed his fingers along her arm, and always before kissing her, slid a hand over her cheek, his eyes sparkling as if utterly delighted to discover her there.

To know that they had their years of friendship with something new added on—

It was a magic Madison hadn't expected.

She and Ryan still hadn't discussed where all this was going and what changes she was willing to make to her plans so they could try being together. But there was enough currently on their plates, including needing to figure out Talia's birthday party dilemma, without adding more to today.

Madison figured there was enough time between Christmas and New Year's for the more serious conversation about dating and the future.

A tap on her fingers brought her back to the present. Which was seated at Buns and Roses with Yvette beside her, preparing the final cast list for the Not-So-Nutcracker event.

"You're daydreaming," Yvette teased.

No use in denying it. "Sorry. Ready to do the final check?"

"Let's do it."

Rose had sat with them earlier, double-checking the documents against the online records of monies from the donations, and other than a couple of small mix-ups, everything had balanced. Then she'd had customers at the knickknack and flower half of the shop she'd had to tend to, leaving Yvette and Madison to finish the rest of the task.

The cast list was easy to deal with, and then Madison made Yvette go over the script she jotted down one final time. Between the two of them, they had the very basic, very amateur but very fun event in place before lunch.

Madison sent off the emails while Yvette called the woman Josiah had suggested they ask to be narrator. And then they had a celebratory cinnamon bun to congratulate themselves on a job well done.

Yvette's eyes held laughter. "So. Any suggestions on how cats dance? For when I'm choreographing my routine?"

"No suggestions, other than I am very interested in seeing what you come up with." As well as Sonora, another cat.

The older woman had gotten her wish. Which seemed somewhat coincidental—

If Madison wanted, she could go through and figure out

exactly who had voted for what. But if Sonora wanted to make a big enough donation to ensure that she got to participate the way she wanted, who was Madison to complain?

"I suppose," Yvette agreed. "You're going to be busy enough with Ryan."

For a second, Madison thought Yvette was talking about the wild monkey sex they were having until she realized Yvette was referring to their roles in the community event.

They were playing the rag doll boy and girl magically brought to life as a part of the story.

"Josiah's idea, and it was a good one," Madison admitted. "Since I'm kind of the one running the show, having me onstage most of the time means I'm the one who has to improvise if somebody forgets what they're supposed to do."

"It's going to be a lot of fun," Yvette said. Her smile turned evil. "And I can hardly wait to see Alex. I do hope he doesn't get stage fright."

Madison laughed. "So, *you're* the reason he's a dog."

Yvette put a pretend key to her lips, turned it, then threw it away.

Once they were done at the coffee shop, Madison swung by the fire hall.

She was greeted by a chorus of cheers from the volunteers as she paced past in search of Ryan. First, the usual comments, because she was once again wearing the ugly sweater—Ryan had stuck it in the washing machine, and she'd discovered it when she was about to throw in a load.

Next came approval for the email everyone had obviously already opened.

"Good job."

"Is it typecasting to call Mack a rat?" someone asked.

Charity hit the commenter with the back of her hand then grinned as she pointed back toward where the fire engine was parked. "Ryan and Mack are over there."

They both stopped what they were doing the instant she walked into view. Ryan wore his slightly amused *I can't believe you did this* face.

Mack shook his head. "Really? The Rat King?"

She held her hands in the air innocently. "Your loving public has spoken."

"Your loving wife is going to beat your ass on the stage," Ryan added.

"At least practicing will be fun," Mack pointed out. "Plus, *I* am at least a threatening rodent. You, on the other hand, are a doll."

"Awww, I love you, too," Ryan said before turning to Madison. "I suppose this means we need to plan a practice."

"We have time," she promised. "Today I thought I'd put together our costumes, if you're okay with that."

He waved a hand then paused, reaching into his back pocket and pulling out his wallet. "Here."

Madison snorted. "Cute, but no." She turned to Mack. "If you or Brooke need anything while you're getting ready, let me know."

"Will do."

That night after ballet class, when the dancers were assured they would get a chance to perform on stage, Talia was so excited, it took the combined efforts of Madison and Ryan to calm her down.

The fun of making their costumes helped. Talia enthusiastically made huge X stitches with yarn as she helped sew on the clothing Madison had found at the thrift store.

Eventually, it was just her and Ryan. As tempting as it was to get tangled around each other again like they had the entire weekend, they both seemed to understand the need to change pace while Talia was home.

Ryan turned on the TV, pulling Madison down beside him on the couch. "Tomorrow is my day off. We'll work out the performance stuff we need then. Tonight, I just want to hold you."

Madison couldn't argue with that. Sitting close enough she had one leg resting on his, she relaxed into his arms. Fingers linked, hands balanced on top of her hip. Close enough that when he leaned down and pressed his lips to her temple, nothing else moved. Just a warm, comfortable, intimate position that made her feel alive to her very core.

An evening that contrasted perfectly with the belly-aching laughter the next morning as they began to choreograph their rag doll dance.

She had no idea that her best friend had zero ability to do anything except stand bolt upright like a soldier. After the umpteenth attempt to get him to do something other than march across the room, she was getting worried she'd have to do something drastic. "Maybe you should think about being jelly."

"Because this is something people do on a regular basis?"

"Pretend you're a squid? I know—you're an unattended fire hose."

Ryan made another attempt at his rag doll walk, flopping his way across the living room. He eyed her with just a hint of disgust as she covered her mouth and tried to trap her amusement. "What did I do wrong this time?"

"Nothing. Nothing," she insisted. "You do floppy very well."

His lips twitched. "You are hell on the male ego."

Between his expression and his comment, Madison gave up. She laughed, clutching her stomach, working to catch her breath. It took a while, which meant she ended up on the floor.

He sat beside her, sighing heavily as he patted her leg. "There, there. I'm sure we'll get through this somehow."

She wiped the tears from her eyes, rolling so she could catch hold of his arm. "You need to *relax*."

"Do I now?" His tone changed completely. Deeper, his eyes flashing with interest.

"Uh-huh." Madison twisted until she was between his legs. Sliding her hands down his thighs, she leaned toward him and brushed her lips over his cheek to his ear. "Every single muscle needs to *relax*."

He shook his head, twisting so his lips hovered over hers. "What you're doing is making me stiff. Just saying."

"Oh, well, *that* might be a problem." She toppled him to his back, hands braced on either side of his body. "Maybe we do something about that first and then work on turning the proper parts of you to jelly."

She eased away, sliding her palms over the soft cotton of his T-shirt. The muscles underneath were all flexed—he really was hard everywhere. She caught hold of the waistband of his sweats, pulling them down along with his boxers just enough to free him.

Gaze fixed on his, Madison wrapped her fingers around his erection. "I want this."

"It's all yours," Ryan said happily, the last word turning into a groan because she'd immediately dipped her head and wrapped her lips around his hard length.

She worked him slowly. Teasing her tongue along the thick, heavy weight of him. Closing her mouth and sucking hard as she pulled up. Holding him firmly at the base with a grip that flowed up and down, chasing her lips.

The tightness in his body increased. The hand at the back of her head was still gentle even as he encouraged her to keep slow, go deeper.

"Fuck." He curled upright slightly, impressive abs hard at work. His hands now cupping her cheeks. "Close," he warned.

Madison pulled even harder, waiting for the spill of salt across her tongue.

It took three more draws before he lost control. Torso

shaking, hips bucking upward, lips whispering her name. Seconds later, Ryan lay sprawled on his back, breathing heavily, an enormous smile on his face.

It was probably cruel, but it *was* the point she was trying to make. Madison caught him by the hand and pushed to her feet, dragging him with her. "Stand up. Stand up. Right now."

"What?" Ryan rolled, pressed a hand to the ground and stumbled upright. Sweatpants stuck around his ankles, he glanced around as if wondering what the panic was. "What's—? Oh, *hell.*"

She stepped in as his legs briefly caved. Madison smiled as she wrapped an arm around his waist and supported him until he caught his balance. "And that, my dear friend, is the type of leg motion we're going for as rag dolls."

Ryan stared at her for a moment. Shock, then understanding, then amusement spilled out of him. He paused to jerk up his pants then dragged her into his arms and squeezed her tight as he twirled her in a circle and laughed. "Madison Joy. You are one in a million."

14

The parking lot had been nearly full. By the time Ryan finished making sure everything was set up for the night at the fire hall with the replacement volunteers, there was only an hour to go before the performance.

The open area of the Heart Falls Community Centre was already half-full. Some people were chatting, and a group in the corner had spontaneously burst into Christmas carols. A horde of little girls in tutus and three little boys in dance leotards pranced and flounced around the room, enormous smiles on their faces.

Ryan spotted a half dozen people in the audience who seemed to be wearing ugly sweaters—and wasn't quite sure what to do with that discovery.

Instead, he made his way to the front where Rose manned a table, a number of pretty baskets on display, small boxes slowly filling with raffle tickets in front of each one.

"Nearly ready?" he asked.

Rose flashed a thumbs-up then jerked it over her shoulder toward the left side of the stage. "I'm very glad your girlfriend has an artistic flair. I will take care of the donations, and you can go help Madison and Josiah deal with the backstage chaos."

He tried to ignore how his heart skipped at the word *girlfriend*.

At the top of the short staircase, he was met by Josiah. The local veterinarian had a background in stage, although he didn't talk about it much. He was, though, as Madison had described him, "the perfect cohort in crime," because she'd barely had to describe what was supposed to happen and he'd understood and suggested ways to make it better and easier.

Josiah shook Ryan's hand then offered a grin. "I like your Madison. She did a really good job of coming up with something simple but fun."

"Fingers crossed everything goes as planned," Ryan said. He glanced at Madison—who had crossed to the other side of the stage—dipped his chin to Josiah, and made his farewell.

Considering there was a lot of noise and a constant stream of people coming up to her, Madison remained very calm cool and collected. She offered Ryan a wink and then redirected a couple of teenagers toward the music system.

"Any last-minute things I can do?" Ryan asked.

"Definitely." She caught him by the hand and tugged him to the side of the room and through a door.

It wasn't until she shut it that he realized they were in a storage closet. And then he couldn't see what they were storing because she cupped his face with her hands and pulled him in for a scorching-hot, demanding kiss.

His heart was pounding by the time she broke the contact between them. Maddy patted his cheek then reached behind her and pulled the door open.

They were back in the crowd before Ryan had time to do more than light on fire inside.

She grinned evilly. Pointed to the side of the stage where his costume was draped over the back of the chair. "Get ready. It's nearly showtime."

How had he been talked into this? Right, this was *Madison*. She could talk a ground squirrel into buying real estate beside a coyote den.

Familiar faces were everywhere, but Ryan stayed in the shadows, waiting for the performance to start. Charity had Talia and the other dancers under control, so now it was time to enjoy the mischief Madison had created.

As the stage darkened and the room quieted, Madison stepped beside him. Her fingers linked with his.

The clear, brisk voice of the Heart Falls elementary school principal sounded over the loudspeaker. Ivy Stone might not like to be the center of attention, but hidden offstage where she could see but not be seen, she was the perfect narrator.

A single light shone on the empty stage, and Ivy began.

"Welcome to the Not-So-Nutcracker performance for Heart Falls. Because this is a magical story, you'll notice we have magical helpers."

People dressed all in black ran onstage. Some carried in the props—two chairs and a table. The others held large pieces of cardboard that Fern Fields had painted as backdrops. These helpers stayed onstage, standing motionless as they held the scenery in position.

"Let's begin. Once upon a time, there was a family who moved to a wonderful, small town. They arrived just in time for the holidays, and their new neighbours brought them all sorts of gifts to make their time in their new home special."

Music swelled in the background as Brad Ford—and his wife, Hanna, carrying their six-month-old, Drew—made their way to the chairs in the center of the stage. A stream of people joined them, each dancing or otherwise making their way into sight. Some walked slowly, some skipped. The town mayor, a tall man wearing a bright-red turban, waltzed in with his wife, who wore a shimmering gold sari.

All of them brought brightly wrapped presents they placed on the small table.

Ryan and Madison also made their way onto the stage, walking straight legged for a few steps before nearly collapsing, as if they didn't have bones in their legs. They finally slid to the ground at the side of the stage near the painted fireplace. Children pointed and laughed, and Ryan's friends visible in the audience flashed thumbs-up.

Madison had pulled her hair up into two pigtails high on her head. Ryan had slicked his into a Mohawk. Madison had bright-yellow sweats as bloomers that contrasted with her bright-pink dress. She'd found Ryan yellow pants as well—*who had bought these in the first place?*—and a red vest nearly as gaudy as their sweater.

The clothes were all one size too big, and with the large stiches sewn on in places, they looked like two well-loved, handmade dolls.

Both of them had black lines that made their mouths look stitched on, with bright-red circles on their cheeks and enormous dark freckles. Ryan had drawn the line at the eyelash makeup until he'd seen what it looked like on Madison.

It looked good. Like they were two fabric creations about to be hit with Christmas magic.

He'd let her draw lashes on him as well.

Ryan let his body semi-collapse, leaning against Madison as they waited for the next part of the story. The lights dimmed slightly, and everyone on stage walked off, taking the chairs, the table, and the presents with them. Only the backdrop holders remained.

While the narration carried on in the background, all of those first performers made their way to the seats reserved down on the main room floor. Now they got to sit back and enjoy the rest of the show as part of the audience.

"Because this was the holiday season, there was more magic floating in the air that night than usual. The rag dolls that had been brought as gifts suddenly came to life."

It was their turn.

Madison held out her hand, and Ryan took it, both rising to their feet. They fell into the script and the few lines they had.

"How is this possible?" Madison turned in a slow circle, raising her hands high, then wiggling her fingers as she stared in wide-eyed delight.

Ryan flopped his way to her side and retook her hand. "Holiday magic makes *anything* possible."

They started their dance. Laughter rose nicely in the right places. Ryan did his best to remember all the bits and pieces that he and Madison had practiced without getting distracted by the other things they'd done during practice to get the weak-kneed sensation just right.

They finished and took their floppy bows to a swell of applause.

"Then, suddenly, out of the darkness, danger arrived!" Ivy's shrill warning pulled a shriek from a few younger members of the audience. Abruptly, Mack Klassen stood on the stage. He held a sword made out of an empty Christmas paper roll high in the air.

"Arrghh."

Laughter rang out, rising even higher as Brad shouted, "You're a Rat King, not a pirate!"

It took a moment for the crowd to catch their breath. All the while, Mack shook his finger at Brad, shaking his head as if he could not believe it.

"'Oh, no,' said the rag doll girl to the rag doll boy. 'We'll be destroyed. Who will save us?'" Ivy raised and lowered her voice as she spoke the dolls' lines. "'We can save ourselves.' 'Not against teeth and claws. And not against so many of them.'"

Mack had been joined by the local Taekwondo group. The dozen students wore little rat ears along with rope tails attached to their outfits. While brisk military fight music played in the background, they went through their forms, all the time scowling and baring their teeth and otherwise attempting to look ferocious.

They finished with a bow to lots of parental cheering.

Ivy raised her voice and brought the event into motion again.

"'No, against teeth and claws, you need more.' It was a deep voice that rang through the house, and the rag dolls looked everywhere.

"'Who said that?' 'Have you come to save us? Are you a soldier?'"

Onto the stage, Brooke swaggered. She shrugged easily. "Nah. What you need here, in Alberta, is the rat patrol." She poked a thumb into her chest. "And I'm the chief rat catcher."

Madison caught Ryan's hand again and spoke up. "It's true. We should have known."

"There are no rats in Alberta."

They nodded like bobbleheads.

The audience was really enjoying themselves, and when the stage cleared—the current crowd sliding to their seats on the sidelines—the fight between the Rat King and the Rat Catcher began.

Mack and Brooke had obviously had fun putting their scene together. They thrust. They parried. They chased each other, Mack after her, then Brooke after him. Suddenly, while the Rat King continued to race in circles, the Rat Catcher stopped and scratched her head.

She wandered to the side and held up a hand as if she'd had an idea. Then she took a deep breath. And another, as if bracing for battle. She practiced a few swings of her sword, shook her head, and tried again.

Meanwhile, the Rat King had realized he was no longer being chased. He turned, crept forward slowly, sword raised, ready to strike a blow...

Children in the audience screamed warnings at the top of their lungs. Jumping up and down, they pointed at the Rat King and waved at the Catcher.

Brooke turned just in time, sword slamming into Mack's without a sound—since they were made of cardboard. In fact, Mack's twisted and bent in half, drooping.

Mack looked sadly at his sword before glancing up and shouting, "Clash."

Brooke snorted then straightened. She shouted, "Clang."

By the time the fight was over, the Rat King lay on his back, arms stretched toward the ceiling, feet in the air. Brooke placed a foot on his chest and raised her sword in the air triumphantly.

The audience shrieked with laughter as the second sword also folded into a crumpled mess.

As the silent background people dragged away the Rat King, who waved farewell as he went, Madison and Ryan came forward and shook Brooke's hand.

Ivy's narration picked up again.

"'Thank you for saving us', the rag dolls said politely. The Rat Catcher threw back her head and laughed. 'You're welcome. I always have time to save others. Also, I like company. I live in a magical barn,' she told them. 'If you'd like to visit, come with me.'"

Brooke raced around the front edge of the stage, Madison and Ryan following. The background people changed and held pictures of barn posts and horse stalls along with two real hay bales on the ground.

"Stepping into the magical barn, the rag dolls were amazed

as the most magical thing yet happened," Ivy announced. Amusement tinged her voice. "The chief barn pixie arrived with all his fairy court to welcome them."

Dustin Stone stepped royally onto the stage.

Accompanied by Talia, Emma, and the rest of the little dancers, the man was the youngest of the Stone brothers. In his early twenties, with a sturdy build and dark hair, he wore all-black clothing topped with a silver vest, silver fabric tied at his wrists and the ankles of his stocking-covered feet.

A silver tiara was pushed down on his black cowboy hat.

Madison leaned in and whispered in Ryan's ear so softly, there was no fear of being overheard, especially not with the enormous applause and volume of laughter ringing over the room at Dustin's appearance. "His brothers came in at the very last second and put a thousand dollars over the nearest bid to make sure he won. His nieces designed his costume and choreographed his dance. He's a riot."

His good-natured acceptance of his role was clear, especially when he reached behind him and lifted a silver wand in the air. His nose rose just slightly as if he were royalty allowing the others to partake in his awesomeness.

He waved the wand twice. "Pixies—I command you to do the welcome dance!"

Dustin stepped back, and the little dancers all rushed to get into their positions. Talia's eyes sparkled as she and her friends leapt and pirouetted and had the most wonderful time as pixies. Ryan's heart filled with happiness for her.

Then his gut was full of laughter because, when the ballet group finished, Dustin began. With the help of his nieces, he dipped and swayed then went up on the toes of his cowboy boots the best he could.

Dustin held his arms to the side, eyeing the audience before him. He pressed a finger to his lips, and the crowd hushed.

Another moment of fanfare, then in one quick motion,

Dustin twirled in a circle, completing a fairly decent pirouette. Then he dropped into a crouch with outstretched arms like a vaudeville performer. He turned his back on the crowd and shimmied to make the wings attached to his vest wiggle, and the place lost it.

The rest of the performance was equally fun, including dancing cows that did a can-can line and prancing goats. And yes, Ashton was there onstage.

He'd made himself a longer-than-usual beard and furry grey ears, and their dance seemed to involve a lot of picking up their feet and kicking wildly. When they finished in a tall tower, though, pretending to stand on each other's backs, loud calls of approval rang out.

Yvette was a dancing cat along with Sonora and a couple other women. Then the dogs came out, and their dance seemed to consist of racing in circles and rounding up the other dancers. Alex was there. So was Josiah's wife, Lisa, who wore their teeny baby, Zoë, in a contraption on her chest. A small terrier followed at her heels like a mini shadow and barked every time Lisa snapped her fingers.

Ryan's favourite, though, were the Canada geese who did a kind of RCMP circle dance, the entire time muttering *sorry, sorry, sorry*, as they bumped into each other.

When the final dance was done, Ryan's stomach hurt from laughing.

"But like all magical days, this one had to come to an end. The rag dolls said goodbye to their new friends in the barn and made their way back to the house."

The final performers left the stage, the background people changed, and Brooke led Madison and Ryan back into the house and beside the fireplace.

"'Goodbye', the Rat Catcher said. 'Merry Christmas, and thanks for coming to visit. I think the magic will be fading soon.'"

They all hugged, then Maddy and Ryan settled back on the floor as Brooke threw her hands in the air. The lights went out.

When the lights came back on, Brooke was gone. Only a crash rang out, and something fell in the background. Brooke's muffled *ouch* was loud enough that most people heard it.

"'Do you think we'll ever see her again? Or visit the magic barn?' the rag doll girl asked. 'I think we will,' the rag doll boy told her. 'Magic always comes at Christmas, but sometimes, if we really want it to, it stays all year 'round.'"

"And this concludes our performance of the Not-So-Nutcracker."

Madison's fingers were linked with his. Ryan had his other arm around her waist, and they were leaning on each other, cozy and comfortable. Perfect and right, and Ryan wanted to stay there. In spite of being dressed like a rag doll. In spite of the makeup on his face.

He was with Madison, and that's what made it perfect.

15

The entire household buzzed for days after the performance. Talia was now off from school, which meant Madison got to dive in and enjoy full days with the adorable little girl.

Ryan insisted Maddy didn't need to babysit. "Everything is still lined up with Laura," he reminded her. "And you seem to have found a posse of women to make trouble with. You should spend time with them."

"I'll make sure that I do," Madison promised. "But I'm also enjoying the time with Talia."

The day after the performance was Ryan's full day off, which meant jumping in on solving the problem of Talia's birthday.

Having dealt with her younger brothers over the years, Madison figured there might be some tears and grumbling involved as they worked their way to their final destination. With that in mind, she whipped out some giant Post-it notes in bright colours. "Okay, kiddo. You ready for this?"

Ryan was doing the dishes, but he called over his shoulder, "Make sure you leave room for me. I have ideas, too."

Talia looked at the pile of pens and paper with suspicion. "This looks like homework."

A snicker escaped Madison. "Are you sure you haven't been talking to my little brothers?"

"Not since last week," Talia insisted.

Considering it was only three more sleeps until the little girl's birthday, she'd been amazingly calm, but when she started off the whole thing by reiterating her main point, it was clear she wasn't budging. "I want my birthday on my *birthday*. Please, Daddy?"

Ryan nodded. He dried his hands then grabbed one of the giant notes and wrote in bold letters. "Celebrate Talia's birthday on December twenty-fifth." He ripped the page off the pad and handed it to her. "Stick it on the wall as high as you can reach. That's our goal. Everything underneath will be ideas or maybes."

Madison eased back in her chair. "Wow. I don't even need to be here."

"Yes, you do," Talia complained as she rushed back to the table and grabbed Madison's arm.

"Oops. Sorry, sweetie, I wasn't talking about leaving. I was talking about your daddy knowing exactly what we're doing with the notepads."

"Maddy, after all the times you made me study and brainstorm using this method, nothing will ever erase it," Ryan said dryly.

The end of that small interplay had Talia sitting in Madison's lap. The little girl's scent and the way she rubbed her hand over Madison's arm made the box of hope inside her chest crack open even more.

Madison was pretty sure she'd fallen in love with Ryan. But she was completely certain Talia had stolen her heart from the minute she'd walked in the house.

Time to focus. "What things would make your birthday special?"

For the next twenty minutes, they wrote down everything from the simple to the ridiculous. Which meant they spent a lot of time laughing, Talia rolling her eyes as her daddy wrote down things like "ride on kangaroos" and stuck them on the wall.

But excitement slipped in along with the perfect solution when Ryan paused in the middle of a Google search. "I think I've got it."

Talia ran to his side and, with his help, read the article that said in some cultures, the birthday girl would be the one to hand out presents.

Talia thought for a moment. "If I make things for my friends, and we go to their houses, then we won't be interrupting their Christmas with their family. Maybe?"

She turned wide eyes upon Ryan then glanced over at Madison.

If she had to spend hours phoning all of Talia's friends to figure out a schedule that would work, so be it.

While Ryan and Talia worked on the list of people she really wanted to celebrate with, Madison brainstormed a few ideas of simple gifts that Talia could be involved in making.

In the middle of it, her brother called. Madison slipped from the table and went and stood by the window, looking out over the snow-covered yard. "Hey, Kyle."

"Hey, Mad. Wanted to let you know the gift box you ordered for mom arrived. I distracted her, and Joe got it wrapped up and under the tree."

"Thanks, guys, that's awesome." She could just picture the holidays at home. The familiar decorations, her mom bringing out the fancy cookie cutters she only used at this time of year. "I'm going to miss you turkeys," Madison admitted.

"Miss you, too. Only, sounds as if you're having a good time with your friend."

"Definitely. Today we're planning a birthday party." Madison glanced down to discover Talia standing in front of her with her hand out. "Yes?"

"I want to talk to your brother. Please?" Talia pulled her hand behind her back and stood there looking devilishly cute.

Madison laughed. A week ago Talia had caught her chatting with Joe and taken over the phone. By the end, both Joe and Kyle had been on speaker phone, telling Talia stories and making the little girl giggle.

It had turned Madison's heart inside out to hear it.

So now, she was pretty sure what kind of a response she'd get from her brother. "Hey, Kyle. Talia would like to talk to you again. You got time?"

"Sure. She's a sweetheart."

"Here she is. Love you, bro."

Talia took the phone very politely and then stepped to the side and began immediately sharing all of the plans for the travelling birthday party that would be happening on Christmas Day.

Madison returned to the table and sat beside Ryan.

He slipped his hand over hers and squeezed. Close, connected. "You raised some good kids."

"You're not doing a bad job yourself," she said, turning to him. Face so close, body right there. It would be so easy to lean in and press their lips together. So right, yet not what she was allowed.

Excitement bubbled out of Talia as she zipped back to where they sat and handed the phone to Madison. "Kyle has an idea," she all but shouted.

Madison went back to her brother. "What's up?"

"In case it helps, Talia said she needs a present to give to all her friends. You remember when we made cookies in a jar?

Everybody we gave them to loved them, and Joe and I had a blast making them."

It was perfect. "Kyle, you're a genius."

"Of course I am. Got raised by the best big sister in the world."

Talia danced around the room while Madison updated Ryan on the idea.

It was Ryan who added another brilliant touch. "If you don't think it's too weird to have people help make their own presents, Talia could have Emma and Chrissy come here to make up the cookie jars."

Which is how, on Wednesday afternoon, the house was filled with Talia's friends for a not-birthday-party but a get-ready-for-a-party event. Which probably wasn't much different from what her actual birthday would've been, but Talia was happy, which made Ryan happy.

Which made Madison want to straight up tell him that she planned on never leaving.

They set up stations around the island in the kitchen. Ryan did the tricky part of putting flour, salt, and baking powder into the bottom of the jar. Then he passed it to Talia, who got to scoop in chocolate chips and sugar. Crissy added nuts. Emma topped it off with coconut.

At the end of the line, Madison closed the jars with the festive piece of fabric she'd found that had balloons on it. A piece of ribbon around the neck held the directions for assembly and baking.

When the girls raced off to play in Talia's room, Ryan stepped in behind Madison, sliding his hands over her hips and tugging her back against his body. A full-length, backwards hug as he just stood there and rocked them quietly. His cheek against hers as they admired the collection of jars all over the table.

"Thank you for making another special memory for my daughter." Ryan caressed his lips over her ear.

"Making good memories for me as well," Madison pointed out.

It was tempting to turn. To wrap herself up tight in his embrace and admit what she was feeling. Instead she stood there and soaked in the moment of gratitude he offered. The connection of two good friends making memories for a little girl.

Christmas Day just continued the fun.

While Talia had insisted it was her birthday, more than birthday presents rested on the table in the morning.

Madison shrugged. "I brought some things with me."

"And I had already picked up some stuff as well," Ryan admitted.

Talia leaned forward, interest rising when she noticed her name on one of the boxes. "I don't mind *sharing* Christmas with my birthday."

Ryan laughed until he cried when the far-too-small to be suspicious box with his name from Madison on it turned out to hold a note that read "under the table." He peeked and discovered she'd stuck the sweater to the underside with some sturdy duct tape.

The delivery of Talia's birthday gifts took a lot longer than Madison expected. Thank goodness Ryan had stepped in and taken over making the schedule, because Madison had assumed they'd come to the door, Talia would shout *happy birthday*, explain what she was doing, and then they'd leave.

Madison had forgotten to factor in that, unlike her brothers —who would have been focused on conquering the list—Talia was a social butterfly. Ryan planned the visits for when friends said they would be on a break from their own Christmas celebrations, which meant every place they stopped issued an invite to join in for a drink or treat. So much good food, and so many wonderful people.

Hanna and Brad had a bonfire going in their backyard, so they stopped to roast a marshmallow and make s'mores. Little Drew's eyes were wide as flames flickered in front of them.

Out at Silver Stone ranch, Emma's extended family was all out in the arena, riding. Emma and her big sister, Sasha, immediately took Talia off into the goat pen, where laughter rang out in loud peals over and over.

It was nearly five o'clock by the time Ryan, Talia, and Madison got home, and Talia was still bouncing. "Suppertime now. Yes?"

Ryan tousled her hair and grinned. "Yes. It's time for your birthday pizza."

It was un-Christmassy in so many ways, yet all the touches were there that Madison needed for her own celebration. She talked to her mom and her brothers. She'd stopped in and visited with all of her new friends.

She'd watched Talia's eyes dance with happiness as she presented canning jars full of cookie mix to all of the special people in her life, including her ballet teacher and, "Ms. Sonora, who takes care of all the puppies."

And when Talia went to bed, Ryan caught Madison by the hand and pulled her into his bedroom where he locked the door and proceeded to give her another very wonderful, very appreciated gift.

He undid the buttons of the red sparkly sweater and carefully placed it on the chair. "Wouldn't want anything to happen to that. I'm pretty sure you'll be wearing it at least once more this month."

Madison smiled as he moved in and pressed their lips together, connection and pleasure sliding in. He stripped away her clothes and his and brought her onto the mattress. Working his way down her body then teasing her until she shook with need.

Then he rolled her on top of him, handed her a condom, and put her in charge. Which was just fine. Perfect in fact.

She took her own turn exploring his body. Kissing and licking and appreciating every one of his muscular contours. Easing the condom on slow enough, his thigh muscles all but quivered by the time she rose over him and rocked her sex on his hard length.

One inch. Another. Slowly she joined them together. Hands pressed to his chest, his fingers digging into her butt cheeks as he shook with need.

"Feels so good." The words slid from him, deep and rasping.

"Going to feel better," she promised. Rising slowly, following down. Filling and emptying over and over. Speeding up as the need rose and his hands took control. Helping keep her in position as he thrust up into her.

Ryan slid one hand forward, between her legs. Stroking where he entered her body, intimate and so very good. His fingers wet, he dragged moisture over her clit. Rubbing hard enough that there was no stopping, no slowing down.

Pleasure wrapped around both of them and exploded. Bright lights flared like fireworks at the edges of her vision.

She wasn't falling. She'd landed.

Madison was in love with her best friend, and the only way to make it better?

Make it last forever.

16

Because they'd used Friday for Talia's special day, Saturday meant a trip to Black Diamond for a holiday meal with his parents. Plus, Talia was lined up for an extended visit for a few more days.

His daughter hauled Ryan into her room for a private talk as she packed her bag for the trip. Turning her serious little-girl eyes on him, she folded her arms over her chest. A mirror image of him. "I want to stay with Nâinai and Yéyé, but I want to stay here with Madison, too."

"I know. Only, your grandparents have been looking forward to time with you."

Talia's lower lip quivered, and she sighed mightily. "I'm happy about staying with them, but I feel like crying."

"Oh, little one." Ryan pulled her into his arms and held on tight. Teenage Talia was just around the corner. He'd need divine intervention to survive the coming storm, and yet he couldn't wait.

Learning who this tenderhearted yet bold child would grow into thrilled him to bits.

By the time he and Madison were getting ready to leave

Black Diamond, his daughter was once again smiling. He noticed she gave both he and Madison equally long, possessive hugs before they left.

He had to agree. Letting Madison go when it came time would be hell on both Talia and him.

Ryan and Madison returned to Heart Falls and dove into a very long and enthusiastic Saturday night crowd at Rough Cut.

Since he didn't have to go pick up Talia, Sunday became a catch-up day. Madison vanished for a few hours with her new girlfriends. When she returned, her cheeks were glowing from the cold.

She also had a snowball hidden in her hand that she shoved down the back of his shirt seconds after sliding back into the house.

He retaliated by stripping her down right there and taking her on the living room floor. Their laughter shifted into moans and cries of pleasure that echoed off the walls of his home.

Ryan had her in his bed, and his arms, every chance he got since they didn't need to worry about Talia walking in on them.

The sex was amazing, but interestingly, Ryan found himself simply holding Madison for long moments at a time. Walking up behind her in the kitchen. Interrupting her as she pulled on her coat. Spooning around her in bed, legs impossibly tangled together. As if storing up the connection between them would somehow help him survive once she was gone.

A dozen times he'd opened his mouth to ask if she would consider changing her plans. Stick around and stay close instead of moving to the other end of the country.

Each time, Ryan stopped himself. It wouldn't be right. She'd done it before without anyone asking. Simply given up everything she was working toward to give to others, and while she'd said it was what she truly wanted, he refused to put her in that position again.

He tucked the ugly sweater into the chip box high in the

pantry cupboard in the hopes they'd have one final laughing discovery before she said goodbye.

One last shot at their sweet, wild tradition, and he let the sadness rise but felt contentment at doing what was right. He'd miss her. Talia would miss her. But Madison deserved her chance to bloom.

Monday he had day duty at the fire hall. Madison hadn't joined him this time. Ryan had to admit that he'd woken up on the grumpy side of the bed. Which was wrong on so many levels.

He had time alone with Madison, and yet here he sat, grumbly as a bear that'd had his honey taken away. It was just not right.

Alex paced into the large common room of the fire hall, took one look at him, then collapsed into the nearby chair with a grin. "Did you get a lump of coal in your Christmas stocking?"

Ryan blinked. "What?"

"So sad." With a shake of his head, Alex rose to his feet and went to the fridge, returning with two water bottles. He dropped one in front of Ryan then cracked open his own and took a long swig before pointing the top toward Ryan. "You have it bad."

Okay, now Ryan was edging past cranky and into full-out pissed. "Stop with the cryptic bullshit."

"Hey, no need to get snarky. I'm serious. Although, I suppose the phrase should actually be *you have it good*."

"Alex, I'm going to hurt you." Ryan said it as dryly as possible even as he considered if, for some reason, a down and dirty fistfight was what he needed right now.

His friend's expression changed. Amusement slid away and was replaced by...confusion. "Tell me you're smarter than this. Tell me you aren't ignoring the fact that you're in love with Madison."

A dry hack escaped Ryan's lips. "Excuse me?"

"You know, the curvy redhead who's been your shadow for the past month? The woman from your past who brightens your every day. Yada, etc., blah, blah, blah."

If his water bottle had been only slightly emptier, Ryan would have hurled it at Alex's head. "Stop with the nonsense. Madison and I aren't in love."

"Sorry, not nonsense." Alex shrugged. "You're not that good of an actor. I know you two have been hitting the sheets for at least a couple weeks. You walk around with a perma-grin instead of being Mr. Calm, Cool and Barely Breathing."

It was none of his friend's business, but for some reason, Ryan needed to admit part of that was true. "Yes, we're having sex. Great sex, which if I seem to remember, *you're* currently not enjoying."

"Ouch, low blow, man." But Alex still wore a grin. "So the hormones are hopping enough to make you ignore the other bit that's happened to fall into place when you were otherwise busy...and you can take that *busy* any way you want."

"We're not in love," Ryan insisted, truly exasperated now. "Love hits hard and fast and makes you dopy and light-headed—"

Alex cut him off with a snort. "You're lucky you didn't walk into traffic if that's what falling in love the first time did to you."

"There is nothing other than the first time," Ryan repeated. "That's what I'm telling you."

"Yeah, right." Alex glared at him now. "You know what? Lie to yourself all you want, but maybe you should think about Madison. Considering she's supposed to be your best friend, you really shouldn't treat her like this."

"I'm not in love—" Ryan cut off in the middle of his shout. Because yes, that's how bad it was. He was shouting at a friend while inside, his gut ached and all he wanted was to take Maddy into his arms and tell her to stay with him. This thing was making him all fucked up inside, but somehow, he and Madison would figure it out.

Damn. Ryan had said that last bit out loud, and now Alex was staring at him. Total judgement on his face.

"Ha—hard to figure it out when the woman is headed a couple thousand kilometers away from you." Compassion slid into Alex's face. He lifted his chin. "Hey. I'm sorry. Maybe I'm picking up something that's not there because I know *I* can't start something right now with someone I'm interested in. So interested that I hope it might lead to forever, but my hands are tied. Yours aren't."

The shift was enough to knock Ryan off denial and into a spiral of truth. He knew he wanted Madison to stay. He'd admitted as much to himself.

Was it...*love*?

Alex cleared his throat. "Well, now that I've firmly put both boots in my mouth, let me finish with this. Maybe you don't know that you're in love. Maybe you don't know if she's in love with you, but one thing can't be ignored. It's easier to figure that shit out when you're in the same area of the country."

His friend rose, pausing only long enough to place a hand on Ryan's shoulder and squeeze firmly before walking into the back of the hall.

Ryan couldn't move. Was he...in *love*...with Madison Joy?

He shook his head. Couldn't be. He'd fallen in love before, and it hadn't been like this at all. This time there'd been no rush of energy, no babbling or wanting to stare into her eyes every moment...

It wasn't the same as it had been with Justina. Maybe he should ask Madison if she knew—

Ryan collapsed back in his chair. Right. Ask Madison. His first response was so not a good idea.

The warning siren went off overhead, and all mental

wrangling was pushed aside in the rush of emergency response.

Hours passed as they worked to contain a fire at a nearby ranch. The outbuilding that had gone up was old and shaky, and far too close to the new barn full of animals.

Icy-cold wind and a pumper truck made for a freezing battle mixed with hellish heat as they moved between the flames and outside, helping the owners get the animals out of danger.

Ryan had no time to be distracted, but strangely, the peace he felt every time he pictured Madison at home, waiting for him, was what made it through his thick head.

It wasn't giddy, bubbling love like the first time, but it sure was more than friendship.

The instant he got back to the fire hall, he grabbed his phone.

A voice mail waited from Madison. Somewhere between her phone and his reception, the message was crap.

"...trouble. Don't worry, I'll take......hit the road now. Heard about the fire......later."

Ryan stared at the phone, shocked. Hit the road? She was leaving now? *What the hell?*

He shoved past Alex. "Sorry. I can't stay for cleanup. I gotta go."

"Uh." Alex caught his arm. "Hey, everything okay?"

"No, but it will be."

It had to be.

Ryan tried calling three more times en route home, and every time he went to voice mail, he hung up.

Her car wasn't in the driveway. Fuck. She wasn't supposed to leave for days. How was he supposed to fix this if she wasn't there to help him?

Jamming the truck into park, he called her again, but this time left a message.

"Maddy, when you get this, call me. I know you've got plans, but I love you." He snorted right into his phone. "And that was me being very subtle and blurting it out, but it's true. Call me when you've stopped for the night. Let me come and join you so we can talk about this. Please, let me find a way to make it so we can be together and you can still have your dreams. I love you, Madison Joy. I need you in my world."

He didn't want to hang up. Just sat there staring at the phone until the message stopped recording.

Somehow he made it to the front door, pushed it open, and—

"Daddy!" Talia slammed into him like a bomb, squeezing tight then pushing away with an *ick* noise. "You're very stinky."

"You okay?" It was Madison.

It...was *Madison*?

She was there in his front foyer, bright-purple socks on her feet, the ugly sweater on her body. The entire house was lit up and smelled like pumpkin pie spice.

Ryan kissed her. Caught her by the hand, jerked her against him, and put every bit of what he felt—even if he wasn't able to name it—into the motion.

Right there in front of Talia, who giggled madly.

When he finally released her, Madison eyed him cautiously. Her gaze darted to Talia then back up before she wrinkled her nose. "You do stink."

Oh God. Laughter wanted to rise because she was still there, but—

"What happened? Why is Talia home?"

"Yéyé got sick, Daddy." Talia slipped her hand into his and tugged to get his attention. "Madison came and got me."

"I left you a message," Madison said. "Your dad's okay. His blood levels spiked or something, so they wanted to keep him at the hospital overnight for observation. Your mom called and asked if I could get Talia. She's doing okay but didn't want to have to worry about Talia as well as your dad. I offered for her to come home with us, but she wanted to stay close."

Ryan's heart rate was slowly coming back to normal. He held Talia's hand and still had an arm around Madison's waist. "Okay. Okay."

"You should grab a shower." Madison nudged him toward his bedroom. "Really."

"Not yet." He was going to do this now before he missed his chance. "Talia, I need to talk to Madison. Can you go play for a little while?

His daughter looked up at them, calculated for a moment, then asked, "Are you going to kiss her again?"

Madison glanced up at the ceiling, her lips pressed together like she was trying hard not to laugh.

"Because if you're going to kiss her, you really need a shower first. That's what Crissy's mommy says when her daddy comes home after a fire."

Talia said it bluntly then stole away to the living room and went back to building the 3-D puzzle they'd obviously been working on while they waited for him to come home.

That was it. This was *home*, not because it was where he lived, but because it was where Talia was, and now, where Madison was.

If he could convince her to stay.

Right or wrong, he was going to do it. Somehow he'd find a way to make her happy.

Ryan pulled Madison toward the hallway, stopping in clear view of his daughter. "I need to tease my boss about what things are being said in front of little ears."

"You *kissed* me." Madison ignored his smart comment and went for the main point. "What's going on?"

He hesitated only for a second before diving in. "You're my best friend, and you always find a way to fix what's broken. I need your help."

She frowned. "What broke?"

"Me? Maybe?" Ryan took her fingers and pressed them to his chest. "I don't know how to tell you how I feel without maybe messing up your plans. And I never want to be the guy who stole your dreams."

Her cheeks were turning pink. "How do you feel?"

"Confused, but I've been informed all the signs are there." Ryan took a deep breath. "I'm in love with you, Madison Joy."

Her eyes widened, and her smile—not just her lips but her entire face and body—glowed with happiness. "That's very convenient, because I happen to be in love with you as well, Ryan Zhao."

A small body slammed into the two of them. Talia, no longer on the far side of the room but clinging to both his and Madison's legs. "Is Madison staying? Are you staying?"

The words were muffled as Talia pressed her face to them, but clear enough.

Ryan started, "We weren't done talkin—"

"Yes, I'm staying." Madison bent and hugged Talia, dropping a kiss on her nose. "Now, please, your daddy and I need grown-up talk time. I promise we'll tell you everything you need to know once we're done."

"Okay." Talia wrapped her arms around Madison in a chokingly tight embrace. "I'm glad you're staying."

When they were alone again, Ryan pulled Madison against him. He had no choice, simply had to hold her.

"You have a job to go to," he reminded her.

"It was a job they gave me because my last job vanished. I'm not frothing at the bit to go or following some dream opportunity. I'll explain more, but I'm pretty sure I can sweet-talk the local barkeep into hiring me, *if* I decide that's what I want to do." Madison stroked her hands over his chest as if unable to believe they were there, holding each other.

"I thought you wanted a new start. A brand-new life."

She laughed softly, shaking her head. "What do you think this is? Falling in love with you, moving to Heart Falls. Making friends, helping you raise Talia. Those are all new, wonderful adventures I *want* to have. Perfectly ordinary things that are extraordinary because they're the right things for me. For us."

"Really?"

"Really." She leaned up on her toes and pressed a kiss to his lips. "Please, go shower."

He grinned. "Sorry."

17

That night, after Talia had been convinced sleep was not an optional activity, Ryan led Madison into his room and locked the door.

She eyed him. It seemed once he made up his mind, he was able to be very decisive. Still…

"Nope." He brought her to beside the bed. The one it turned out she'd bought for *them*. "Not waiting. Talia is old enough and has enough friends with two parents to know that people who love each other *sleep* with each other."

"Not a problem. Just a heads-up that the 'sleep with each other' questions are going to get more explicit during the next few years, and I've already explained the birds and bees once. In duplicate."

Ryan moved in close and undid her first buttons. "Then you'll be a great assistant when it's needed."

There and then, Ryan needed zero assistance. He took his time, baring them both and bringing up the need between them. She'd come once before he pulled her into his lap and joined them together.

Intimate. That's what the act was. Also, sweet yet dirty, need and aching trust. And at the core, always, laughing friendship.

Pleasure spiked as Ryan rolled them to the mattress and pushed into her again. Madison clutched the bedsheets and let out a soft moan.

"So good," he breathed quietly then paused, skipping a beat. "Oh, hell, *too* good."

His gaze never left hers, but the tightening of his expression said he was on the edge. Her too. Madison clenched around him and watched him tumble over. A moment later she joined him, pleasure stretching through her. This was her best friend, her lover.

Her love.

They ended up flat on their backs, the bedsheets a mess. The quilt was on the floor, the top sheet barely clinging to a corner of the mattress.

Fingers tangled between them.

Madison rolled, admiring the lean, muscular beauty of the man she planned to spend the rest of her life with.

Which was not the official agenda a few hours ago.

She stroked a hand over his hard thigh. Because she wanted to, because she could. "There's a lot to do tomorrow. Check on your dad. I'll need to call my job and tell them I quit."

"Talk to both my parents. And your Mom. And your brothers."

"What are we supposed to tell them?"

"That we're madly in love, and we'll be getting married, so we should save a date."

Madison blinked. "Married?"

Ryan's smile was slightly cocky but very satisfied. "When it's right, it's right."

Well, she could agree with that, but...

She eyed him. All the long, sexy length of him barely covered with the sheet. "You know, sometimes it's a good thing to *ask* before you blurt out announcements everywhere. Just in case."

He teased his fingers up and down her bare arm, the back of his knuckles casually caressing the side of her breast. "Okay. You're right."

She waited, but he didn't say anything else.

A grin slipped onto her face. "Do you want *me* to propose? Or are you going to set up a fancy evening and do it then? Just wondering, because that *okay* kind of threw me."

Ryan pulled her fingers to his mouth. Kissed her knuckles then spoke softly. "This holiday season has been one revelation after another for me, and I need you to know that I'm grateful."

"Are we still talking about getting engaged?"

"A little." He curled upright and brought her with him, hands together. Still naked, like the truths he shared. "I thought traditions were there to keep us happy. But you've helped in so many ways by messing up traditions on every level."

She wanted to laugh, but his expression was so serious, she held it in.

Ryan shook his head and raised his hand, two fingers in the air. "In one fell swoop, you combined a ballet recital and a fundraiser. The Not-So-Nutcracker was perfect for our community and made a lot of money in a short time. The Hope Fund is full for this coming year because of you messing up tradition."

He lifted another finger. "Talia's untraditional birthday party. I enjoyed our Christmas Day/birthday celebration more this year than I have any year since Talia was born." Another finger. "You made me buy a bed."

This time the laugh did escape. "Beds aren't traditional?"

"Actually, this was the reverse. What I was sleeping on *wasn't* traditional. That single bed was the right thing for me for a long time. But here's where I need to make a confession." He met her gaze. "I think part of the reason I never got a new bed was I'd have to move on. Did I want somewhere I could bring a lover? A potential love? I wasn't ready for that."

Now she was torn between laughter and tears. "Justina will always be a part of our lives."

"A good part," he agreed. "But she'd be the first to tell me *you're* who I need to focus on now. Alive, and sexy, and so willing to give to others—you give me hope."

The sentiment sent her heart pounding.

She caught his hands and pressed a kiss to his fingers. "My NDA—if you and I are officially an *us*, I can tell you now. I caught my boss embezzling. Found a way to let the bar owner know, and it triggered a bunch of stuff that basically means the CEO gave me my notice plus three months' pay and a job in Toronto."

"Getting you out of the limelight?"

"He's shutting down the place for six months and starting over with an entirely new crew."

"Wow." Ryan's expression was sheer amazement.

"Right? Rich people do weird stuff." She had to say it. "And lonely people do things that can't continue. Not if we're going to fix everything that's wrong in your life."

He hesitated. "Okay?"

She brushed her lips over his first to ease the sting of the words she still had to say. The thing that had felt off when she'd tried to figure out Ryan's life had finally become clear. "You didn't buy a new bed because you weren't ready to move on. And you've filled your days with activities you love, but to the point where there's no room to notice how quiet your world is."

"Have you been around my daughter? *Quiet* is not the word I'd use." But he nodded, understanding flooding in. "Holding down two full-time jobs isn't going to work anymore, is it? I want time with you, and Talia, and as a family."

Peace rolled in. *Finally*. Plus, it was her turn to say it. "Okay."

He grinned and tugged her toward him.

Madison held him off. "So can we go back to your *let's get married* comment?"

"If we decide it's right. The tradition-raised core of me says *yes*, but I won't love you less if we skip the ceremony. We should pick the parts of getting married we want and do them with joy. We'll figure out becoming a family in the same way. My job, yours. What we do in the end might not look the same as other families, but it'll be what's right for us, and that's what counts."

Sounded pretty perfect to her.

"Challenge traditions, but don't throw them away without putting something better in place." She leaned toward him, angling for another kiss. "I think we can do that."

"I know we can." Ryan rolled her under him, his grin widening. "We're ordinary people doing extraordinary things. That makes us heroes of our own stories."

She snickered. "That was really cheesy."

"Still true."

He leaned down and kissed her. The one thing she could totally agree on?

Their future would be extraordinary.

EPILOGUE

November 15, one year later.

Alex Thorne sank into a chair in the small coffee shop in the town where he'd grown up. With a deep inhale and an even deeper exhale, he relaxed his shoulders and reached for his coffee.

He was finally able to go home. His *new* home.

Alex didn't regret having gone to his family's rescue. He did regret having to leave Yvette back in Heart Falls without saying something about what she meant to him. What he *hoped* she could mean to him.

Now after being away for so long, he'd be back in Heart Falls in a couple of weeks. Just in time for the holidays, which meant it was a perfect time for him to do the next thing when it came to Yvette as well.

With his upcoming return, setting up a little advance work seemed prudent. He'd been in touch with his friends at the fire hall and Silver Stone over the past months. None of them had mentioned Yvette getting involved with anyone new.

Heck, Ryan had come right out and updated him on a

regular basis, usually with a "get your ass in gear before you lose her" vibe to the notes.

Alex had no idea why he was so fixated on the idea of Yvette, but he'd given up trying to convince himself to look elsewhere. Just like his father before him, it seemed Alex had fallen in love and that was it.

While he didn't want to be creepy about it, he did plan on convincing Yvette that they belonged together. Which required finding a non-creepy way to let her know he was coming back and coming for her...

Yeah, no. That still sounded creepy. Alex dropped his head into his hands and grumbled his annoyance.

He spotted a display of Christmas gifts on the nearby shelf, and slowly an idea grew...

Yvette Wright paced the distance to her country mailbox, focus torn between the text message on her phone from her work at the veterinary clinic and the email update from her grandparents' senior home.

She deliberately shoved her phone into her pocket and forced herself to look around and enjoy the crisp winter day. December was just around the corner, and at some point, she'd have to get into the holiday spirit.

Her plan to settle into Heart Falls had been hugely successful in so many ways. She adored working with Josiah at the Heart Falls Animal clinic. She'd been welcomed in by the local ranchers—not always the case when old men in the ag community and a younger woman making them spend money interacted.

Her grandparents had welcomed her in with open arms, and while her grandpa grew more fragile and forgetful all the time, Yvette was glad to be able to be there with them.

She had girlfriends and volunteer activities…and she was lonely.

Yvette mindlessly flipped through the envelopes in her mailbox. Bills, sale flyers, what looked like a few overeager Christmas letters. Way to make the rest of the world feel like slackers. One was probably from—yup, there it was—postmarked from her sister.

And one envelope, oversized and bulky. Like those Bubble Wrap ones meant to protect the contents. Addressed to her in a fancy script. From—

Alex Thorne?

What on earth?

She'd thought about the gruff cowboy more often than she should have over the past months. That fact was annoying to say the least. They'd never gotten along, always argued…

She'd been terribly attracted to him and fighting it the entire time.

What was he sending her?

Curiosity won out, and she stopped right there on the snow-covered road to tear the top off the envelope and peek inside. No papers.

She tipped it over, and a small, shiny object fell into her hand. A key ring holding a small key and a cardboard disk. The decorative Christmas tree on the end of the chain had little sparkling gems as decorations. It was cute; it was whimsical.

It made her smile *and* shake her head. *Alex, what are you up to?*

The disk had a short handwritten note.

December 1. Buns and Roses, twelve p.m.

New York Times Bestselling Author Vivian Arend invites you to Heart Falls. These contemporary ranchers live in a tiny town in central Alberta, tucked into the rolling foothills. Enjoy the ride as they each find their happily-ever-afters.

~

Holidays at Heart Falls

A Firefighter's Christmas Gift
A Soldier's Christmas Wish
A Hero's Christmas Hope
A Cowboy's Christmas List
A Rancher's Christmas Kiss

~

The Stones of Heart Falls

A Rancher's Heart
A Rancher's Song
A Rancher's Bride
A Rancher's Love
A Rancher's Vow

~

The Colemans of Heart Falls

The Cowgirl's Forever Love
The Cowgirl's Secret Love
The Cowgirl's Chosen Love

ABOUT THE AUTHOR

With over 2.5 million books sold, Vivian Arend is a *New York Times* and *USA Today* bestselling author of over 60 contemporary and paranormal romance books, including the Six Pack Ranch and Granite Lake Wolves.

Her books are all standalone reads with no cliffhangers. They're humorous yet emotional, with sexy-times and happily-ever-afters. Vivian pretty much thinks she's got the best job in the world, and she's looking forward to giving readers more HEAs. She lives in B.C. Canada with her husband of many years and a fluffy attack Shih-tzu named Luna who ignores everyone except when treats are deployed.

www.vivianarend.com